Sacrifice

Carrie's Story

The Carpenter Chronicles: Book One

Janice Limb Myers

DEDICATION

To Shelby Johnson Carr, our wonderful daughter-in-law, who found her prince charming in our son, David, and has blessed us with three wonderful grandsons. We love you!

Cover Credits
Shutterstock_112828861
Shutterstock_864973

Dear Reader,

Thank you for purchasing this, the first book in *The Carpenter Chronicles*. The Carpenters are a family whose faith in God and Jesus Christ sees them through life's trials and tribulations.

This series contains six books, one for each of the living family members. Just a few snippets about the family:

- John Carpenter died four years ago in a skiing accident in Deer Valley, Utah. He was an accomplished skier.

- Grace Carpenter took over running the family publishing business after John's death and has gallantly fulfilled her role as the matriarch of the family.

- Carrie, Chelsea, Carter and Cassie are John and Grace's natural children. Courtney was adopted into the family at age 7 when her mother-who was a sister to Grace-died. Chelsea and Carter have a unique relationship as they are twins. Chelsea and Courtney work in the family publishing business. Carrie is a journalist in New York and Carter is an architect in San Francisco. Cassie is a novelist.

As each book progresses and others are added to the family, you will see the family tree change. I hope you enjoy the Carpenters as much as I'm enjoying writing about them. I promise good, clean stories devoid of bad language or sex scenes, with characters who acknowledge their faith in God and demonstrate good Christian values in spite of challenges they face.

Happy reading!

Janice Limb Myers

PROLOGUE

Carrie was about to take Pete's arm to walk out together when she noticed the under-butler who had served her the water hovering by her side.

"Excuse me, Miss, but the prince has requested your presence in the drawing room for a few moments."

Pete and Carrie glanced at each other and Pete shrugged, lowering his offered arm.

"Guess I'll catch you some other time," he said. "I hope we meet again, Carrie Carpenter of *The Daily New Yorker*."

"Thank you for tonight. I appreciated the company."

"Oh, believe me, the pleasure was all mine."

Carrie was shown to a much smaller and more intimate room. As she entered, the prince was standing, watching her approach, his eyes burning with that dark intensity that made her shiver. Breaking eye contact, he strode over to an antique mahogany cabinet, opening the doors and removing a decanter.

"Would you care for a brandy?"

"No thank you, I don't drink alcohol."

"Ah yes, the wine at dinner. I noticed you refused it. I wasn't sure if perhaps you just didn't care for it. You don't drink at all?"

"No, not at all," Carrie replied, wondering if refusing the wine had been such a big deal that she had been kept back to discuss it, like being held back by your teacher after class because you were in trouble.

"A soft drink then?"

"No, thank you, I'm fine. Prince …"

"Please, just call me Antonio; there is no need for such formality when we're alone."

He said the words, but he didn't drop his formal attitude. Carrie was nervous, not really sure what was going on, so she began to stroll around the room, examining the décor and artwork on display.

"I'm sorry; I should have explained why I wanted to see you, Miss Carpenter."

"Please, call me Carrie," she said, following his lead.

"I just wanted to thank you for all your help in this matter and let you know that I appreciate your actions."

Carrie whirled around to face him, not really sure what actions he was specifically referring to, but ready to brush them off with a not-at-all attitude. Her eyes went wide and her mouth formed a perfect O, her hand flying to her mouth to cover it as she heard a crashing sound to her right.

Almost afraid to look, she turned and stared at the floor in horror. A burgundy and gold vase that had stood on a mahogany pedestal lay shattered on the marble floor, pieces scattered all around.

"Oh, my goodness," she almost cried. "I am *so sorry*; it must have been the dress. I'm not used to this full skirt…."

"Please, Miss…Carrie…" he almost seemed to savor her name as he spoke it for the first time. "Do not concern yourself so; it is only a trinket, not a precious family heirloom or priceless antique."

"I thought everything in the palace was an antique," she wailed.

"Well, perhaps, but it wasn't an important one. Please, come and sit with me for a moment."

***

Janice Limb Myers

CHAPTER ONE

Less than one week earlier …

Carrie Carpenter replayed in her mind the previous night's phone conversation while packing for her trip to Spain.

"You've got to stop living in a fairy-tale world," Susan, her best friend and confidante, had said. "What was wrong with the last guy? I thought the two of you made a cute couple."

"He's a nice guy, but he's not of my faith. In fact, he's probably as close as you can get to being agnostic without being agnostic. You know I want a Christ-centered marriage."

"Then why not the one before him? Or who was that guy before him? Oh yeah, the one that was the pilot."

"He's a member of my church, but he just doesn't do it for me. And the pilot? Well, he's handsome, he's nice, he's romantic, but I just didn't feel he was the Prince Charming I've always dreamed of. No need to waste time on him. I'm not settling for anybody who isn't Mr. Right. I can't put a finger on it, but the pilot is just … well, Mr. Wrong!"

"Remember that song, 'Lookin' for Love in All the Wrong Places'? Maybe that's the problem. Maybe you'll find your Prince Charming on your trip to Spain. You can fall in love with some tall, dark Spaniard in the next four days, right?" They both laughed.

"You know this trip is strictly business, Suse. And besides, I've got to focus on my work. It's a great opportunity to really make a name for myself as an international reporter."

"Then do me a favor, will you, Carrie? Will you just commit to spending some time on this trip *thinking* about settling for someone who isn't 100% died-in-wool Prince Charming? Really, there's no such thing as a perfect man. If there was, he'd expect you to be the perfect woman! I'm just saying all those fairy tales you read as a kid are just that: fairy tales. If you ever expect to get married, you're going to have to settle for Mr. Almost-Right."

Sigh. "Yes, I'll think about it. But I'm telling you now, I think the perfect man for me is out there, and when I find him, he'll share my faith and also want to get married in the temple. I don't think that's too much to ask."

"Okay. Have a great trip. Get some sleep and don't be late for your flight. Want me to call and wake you up?"

"No, it's going to be way too early for you to be up. I've got two alarms set just in case. See you in four days. Nite."

"Nite to you, too. And don't forget your promise!"

Carrie shifted uncomfortably in her seat and pushed back her thick, blonde hair from her flushed face. She'd been so excited and enthusiastic when she'd boarded the flight at JFK in New York, thrilled that she had been given this assignment that the more senior journalists coveted.

It was Carrie who had been chosen to attend a press conference to be held by the royal family of Spain. At the palace, no less! What she still didn't understand was why she of all the reporters had been specifically requested by the palace to represent her paper.

Now, seven hours after boarding the flight, Carrie was cramped, tired, and restless, feeling grubby and disheveled after the long flight. *The Daily New Yorker* would have happily stretched to premium economy for her first international assignment, as she had already become one of their highest-profile journalists.

However, the more spacious and comfortable Airbus planes that offered the upgrade only flew via Heathrow, adding at least another five hours to the trip. It had been imperative that she arrive quickly, so she had been stuck in economy on a direct flight in a Boeing 757, jammed into a middle seat between two businessmen.

Both men initiated conversation during the flight, but their slightly too-eager scrutiny made Carrie uncomfortable, so she quickly apologized and turned to her laptop, feigning lots of work to accomplish during the flight. *Maybe I should have invested that extra five hours for some space and quiet.* She opened her Spanish ebook to try to learn some basic Spanish in spite of the interruptions of her two row-mates.

"Ladies and Gentlemen, this is the captain speaking. We are now just 20 minutes from landing at Madrid Barajas Airport. Please turn off all electronics and follow the instructions of the flight attendants. We will be landing shortly. Thank you for flying with us today."

Oh, great! Now I have to put my laptop away, and I'm stuck between these two guys. They'll expect me to make conversation with them.

"So will you be staying in Madrid, or are you traveling on?" the man to her right asked. He was dressed in a cheap-looking light grey suit, his paunch hanging over the wide airplane seatbelt, his balding head glistening as the air conditioning struggled to keep the passengers in the cattle-car cool.

"Yes, Madrid is my final destination," Carrie replied, feeling on fairly safe territory for the moment.

"That's a shame. I'm catching a connecting flight to Alicante."

"I'm glad I'm not boarding another plane—I can't wait to get off this one and stretch my legs," she laughed, rotating her ankles in the way she had learned online to ease swelling and prevent blood clots while flying.

"Trust me, you look pretty fit."

The way the man glanced at her legs as he spoke made Carrie squirm, and she struggled to pull her skirt down as far as it would go. She had considered her smart business suit of neat skirt and jacket, crisp white blouse and low heels to be the perfect traveling outfit.

Now, she wished she had worn pants instead, as she hadn't factored in the slight rise of her skirt in the awkwardly shaped bucket seats. Her hemline was now sitting about three inches above her knee, instead of just below it, where it was supposed to be.

The words had been innocent enough, but the undertones were most definitely unwelcome.

"Well, I hope you make it in time," she murmured, her Utah society upbringing not allowing her to be impolite, no matter what the circumstances.

"So do I. I'm attending a property conference; the market's very lucrative for a property developer in Spain at the moment."

He puffed with pride, although from what Carrie knew of the situation, buying property in Spain at present wasn't something to brag about; the country, and therefore the housing market, was in a slump due to a recession. This probably meant he was buying half-finished houses that building companies had to abandon when they went bankrupt or homes handed back to the bank when the occupants could no longer afford to keep them. As far as Carrie could tell, the man was a leech *and* a letch. She smiled wanly at him, hoping her refusal to comment would end this uncomfortable moment. No such luck."

"Are you here on business, or for pleasure?"

"Business, most definitely business," Carrie stated firmly. "I'm a journalist for *The Daily New Yorker*."

She couldn't help but smile as she said those words. The position was still new enough for her to feel a great sense of wonder and awe at being a journalist, representing a New York paper right out of college and graduate school, rather than starting out in a smaller town and working her way up.

Taking her smile as encouragement, the man leaned in closer, causing Carrie to retreat as far from him as she could without encroaching on the passenger to her left. "I've heard journalists like to party hard. Is that true?"

"Not this journalist. This is my first international assignment, so I'll be working hard and keeping my mind firmly on the job."

The seatbelt sign was pinging intermittently, and the flight attendants were dashing around, some gathering final, errant pieces of trash while others made their way down the aisles, checking that seats were in the upright positions and all seatbelts were secured. *Please let us land soon,* she begged internally to whoever might be listening.

She longed to look out of the window and see the views, but she knew that leaning toward the obnoxious man on her right would give out signals she definitely didn't want to give. She had never been to Spain; in fact, she had never traveled outside the USA before. From what she had seen online, it was a stunning country, and she was itching for her first glimpse of the mountainous Iberian Peninsula, but it seemed this was going to have to wait until she stepped off the plane.

The man had continued talking, but Carrie had been so lost in her thoughts she had barely paid attention. She smiled at him vaguely, hoping it was enough, assuming he had been talking about himself again. As she felt the plane descend a little more dramatically, her initial excitement, worn down by the drudgery of travel, flared once again. This trip was as much a momentous challenge as it was an opportunity for her.

If she was honest, her family name had secured this position for her. Her father, John David Hinckley Carpenter, had founded and built the very successful and well-known publishing business Carpenter Global Press, which had become even bigger than the name sounded. It was first a local printing business that blossomed into a worldwide publishing powerhouse, considered by many to be one of the 'big four publishing houses' in the world. At least one of her sisters saw it as her ticket to ditching life in Utah and running a large publishing office in New York or London or L.A. once she had some experience behind her.

Although Carrie's name recognition and its significance in the publishing business had provided her an advantage in securing work with major newspapers and given her an edge over her competitors, she knew she would only keep the job on her own merit.

So far, it was all going extremely well. She had quickly settled into life in New York City, working hard to achieve her goals, impressing her superiors at the distinguished broadsheet with her talent and dedication.

If she could keep to that and not let her excitement of an overseas trip distract her or detract from her professionalism, then she would have proved herself beyond any doubt with the assignment.

Finally, the captain's voice came over the speaker system informing them of the local time and immediate weather conditions, thanking them for flying American Airlines, and wishing them a pleasant stay. Carrie fiddled with her watch, adjusting the time setting, waiting for the news she really needed. When the pilot announced that they would be landing at Madrid International Airport in the next few minutes, she felt like applauding.

Carrie followed the crowd of relieved passengers down the tunnel and into the airport. She managed to locate her small case and take the long walk through the corridors to get to the main airport building, where a car had been booked to meet her. By the time she got there, she was thankful for the low-heeled shoes she had chosen to wear and the wheels generously provided by the suitcase manufacturer.

Stepping out of the hectic scene in the building, the heat hit her like the blast from opening an oven door. Intent on not getting lost in the melee, she hadn't realized how cool the building had been. The air smelled fresh and clean despite her current location amid vehicles and exhaust fumes, and the sun was a huge ball of fiery yellow in the perfect blue sky. She was here at last, and it was beautiful.

She was called from her reverie by the sound of her name. She glanced around and spotted a man holding a sign displaying her name and her newspaper's name in bold letters. *I always wanted to see a sign with my name on it when I got off a plane. Now it's happened!* She nodded to him and he hurried toward her, relieving her of her case and the laptop bag she had taken as carry-on luggage.

"Good day, Señorita Carpenter. My name is Miguel Perez, and I am your driver from Executive Travel. Today I will take you to your hotel, if you would like."

"Thank you," Carrie responded, grateful Miguel spoke English, as her Spanish was yet rudimentary.

Carrie trotted alongside the man, glancing sideways at him to take in the details. He was dressed in a grey suit, a blue silk tie complementing the outfit. His dark hair, olive skin, and dark eyes made an appealing package. He was slightly shorter than she was, but he moved with a certain flair and style, as if barely containing unbridled passion. As his highly polished shoes clipped along the paved area, she almost expected him to burst into a fiery flamenco. His heavily accented English merely added to his overall appeal, and Carrie realized she might have a hard time keeping her mind purely on her job if all the men here were as handsome and charming as Miguel.

No, she was here to work, and besides, probably the only men that would show interest in her would be the likes of the aging, balding, brash man from the flight. Her love life, or lack of it, was a bit of a standing joke among her family and friends, both back in New York and in her home in Utah. She always seemed to attract the wrong types, getting herself into pickles with terrible dates. She was too polite to refuse them or to leave a date early, not wanting to hurt her date's feelings. Having lived in New York for a while now, she considered herself to be worldly wise and street smart, but somehow, she was never quite ready for the pushiness of native city dwellers.

She was soon escorted to a black Mercedes E-class, the rear door held open for her. She slid into the seat, the leather almost burning her thighs with the heat from the direct sunlight. Closing her door gently, the driver hurried to jump in the front, turning on the engine and the air conditioning. Cool air blew around her, and Carrie lifted up her mass of wavy hair to cool her neck. Her hair had been in a smart up-do at the beginning of her trip, but it had come loose as it wilted in the heat of the plane, and her head had hurt from the tightly pulled strands and the bulk of it against the headrest. She had soon navigated her way into the tiny bathroom to take it down, unsuccessful in her attempts to tame the tendrils of hair with splashes of water.

She quickly dropped her hair and her pale complexion flamed red as she accidently caught the driver's eye in the mirror. *Idiot*, she scolded herself, *of course he's looking in the rear-view mirror right this minute. He's waiting for a chance to pull out into oncoming traffic.*

She soon forgot her embarrassment when the airport gave way to open land and stunning scenery as they flew along on the 13-kilometer ride to the edge of the city. The vista changed to wide boulevards and breathtaking architecture as they reached the outskirts, then headed toward the center of the city, the driver weaving in and out of traffic at an alarming rate. Soon they were in the very heart of the city center, and Carrie was enraptured by the ambience she could practically feel already. She lost herself in a daydream of sitting at a chic street café in a loose, flowing white dress, sipping a cool drink and watching the nightlife unfold before her. Of course, her workload would be too demanding this trip, but she liked the sophisticated, romantic image she had conjured in her mind.

"I take you to the palace, sí?" the driver asked suddenly, making her jump.

Carrie gulped. "The palace? Oh no." She looked at her slightly disheveled outfit and put a hand to her untidy hair. "I thought we were going to the hotel. The press conference is supposed to be tomorrow!"

The driver laughed—a wonderfully musical tone. "I am sorry, Señorita, I mean the Palace Hotel, not the royal palace, although in the Westin Palace Hotel, you might feel as if you are in a place fit for royalty! It is very luxurious."

Miguel smiled at her in the rearview mirror while Carrie tried to cut through the thick accent and decipher the words. The English was very good, far better than her Spanish, that was for sure, but her ears would take some time to adjust to the differences in the pronunciation. She smiled back at the driver.

"That's a relief! I need to freshen up after the trip; I couldn't meet the prince looking like this!" she laughed. *As if I'm actually going to meet the prince, but at least I'll get to lay my eyes on him. Me and a couple hundred other journalists around the globe. Gee, a girl can dream, can't she?*

"I am sure our prince would be delighted to meet you, no matter the condition of your clothing or hair," Miguel said, punctuating his words with a wink in the rear-view mirror.

Carrie had no idea how to respond. She was used to the warm openness of Utah residents and was beginning to adjust to the sometimes-brash outspokenness of New Yorkers, but she had hardly any experience with other cultures. She didn't know if he was being nice, was flirting with her, or was actually giving her a veiled insult regarding her appearance. She had a feeling she was going to find this culture quite mysterious and intriguing.

"Once again, I see I must apologize. My comment has confused you. I only meant that you are very beautiful, and that even the filthiest of rags would not detract from that beauty."

Oh my goodness, he's making it worse! Is he saying my clothes are filthy rags now? She was incredibly relieved when the car pulled to a smooth stop at the entrance of a beautifully ornate white building. She exited the car, once again feeling the blast of heat as she left the air conditioning behind. She could immediately feel the vibe from the city, historic and elaborate, yet buzzing with a cosmopolitan culture similar to that of New York, except it was all so much cleaner somehow. Miguel closed the door behind her and retrieved her luggage from the trunk.

"Come; let us get out of the sun and this heat."

He made his way to the front of the hotel and Carrie followed, still in awe of her surroundings. Miguel spoke as he walked beside her. "Our firm has been booked for the duration of your stay. Although you are in the heart of the city and close to everything—even the royal palace is only three kilometers away—you must call us whenever you need us."

They had entered the spectacular lobby by now, and Carrie had to concentrate on keeping her mind on what Miguel was saying rather than the sights around her.

He swiftly pulled a business card from his inside jacket pocket and handed it to her. "Do not try to drive in Madrid. The roads and traffic are … how do you say … loco?"

"Crazy is probably the word. Don't worry, I won't. I'll be sure to call. Will you always be the driver?"

"Alas, no, you may have many drivers, but in case I do not see you again, may I wish you a very pleasant stay in our country."

With that, he walked her to the reception desk, placed her bags at her feet, turned, and disappeared out of the building.

"Buenos Dias, Señorita, ¿cómo estás?" asked the smartly-dressed but severe-looking woman behind the reception desk.

"Umm, muy bien, gracias," Carrie replied hesitantly. The woman had been polite, but her overformal smile didn't reach her dark eyes. However, they did flash with understanding as Carrie spoke.

"Ah, you are an American. It is no problem, I speak several languages, and English is one of them."

"Oh, is it that obvious? I'm sorry if I butchered your language, I'm still learning. I wasn't expecting this trip."

The strict woman warmed a little. "Not at all, it was very good. You will find, in this country, if you always speak the little you know, we will always do our best to understand and assist you. Those that try earn our respect. How may I help you today?"

The tone was much friendlier, and Carrie relaxed as they completed the check-in process together.

"Your boss must think very highly of you—you are booked into one of our junior suites," the receptionist said, her smile now genuine and lighting up her dark looks.

"Oh, I don't know about that, but it's nice to know I have a good room. Does it have a bath? I feel so stiff from the flight."

"Oh, we are famous for our trademark Heavenly Beds and Baths. I am sure you will find it the perfect relaxation after your long flight, Ms. Carpenter. Your package includes free Wi-Fi, the pay-per-view movies are complimentary, and you have full access to the gym and spa. Your booking also includes dinner and breakfast at any of our restaurants. My name is Maria and I am here until nine tonight. If you have any questions at all, call me here and I will assist you. José Luis will show you to your room. The hotel is very large, and we would not want you getting lost. You will find a map in the information package on the desk in your suite. Welcome to Madrid, and please enjoy your stay with us."

Carrie was a little taken aback at everything the newspaper had provided for her, but she doubted she would have the time to make full use of the facilities. She made a mental promise to herself that she would return here for a vacation one day, just so she could fully enjoy the amenities and sightsee around this amazing city.

For the moment though, there was nothing else for her to do but thank Maria warmly for her assistance and trot after the bellhop, who had magically appeared at her side, gathered up her luggage, and walked off with it.

Janice Limb Myers

CHAPTER TWO

José Luis escorted Carrie to the elevator and up to the 5th floor to her room. He unlocked the door and held it open for her to enter, then handed her the door key with a flourish. Before she even had time to look for a tip, José Luis disappeared without a word. Carrie was a little surprised. She had made a point to go to the bank and get some small local currency before leaving on this trip, but she wasn't sure of the proper etiquette here toward tipping. Judging by his rapid departure, tipping wasn't expected here, at least not at this hotel. She shrugged, considering his retreat without even saying goodbye a little strange.

Carrie peered around the room, taking it all in with a sense of wonder. Although her family home back in Midvale was a large and impressive house of mansion proportions and French country décor, she had grown used to her small, cramped, and incredibly expensive apartment in New York, almost forgetting how it felt to have a sprawling room stretch out in front of you.

Opening the door leading off the bedroom, Carrie found what she was really looking for right at that moment. A bathroom of marble and pristine white ceramic greeted her. She could hardly wait to enjoy the deep bathtub, but she had to attend to business first.

Walking back through to the living room, Carrie retrieved her laptop and set it up at the desk, plugging it in and using the login information in the welcome packet to connect to the Wi-Fi. Checking her watch, she saw it was just before noon. Her brain was too tired to work out the exact time difference, but she figured it was probably late enough in the morning back in New York to catch her editor in the office; he tended to get a very early start to the day. Using her computer, she dialed the familiar number.

"*The Daily New Yorker*, how can I help you?"

"Oh hi, Julia, it's Carrie. I wasn't expecting you to be in yet. Is Mike around?"

"Hi, Carrie. Yes he's here, I'll put you through."

Efficient as ever, the receptionist transferred her through to the boss.

"Editor," the gruff voice answered. Mike Barrett was a New Yorker through and through, his family going back several generations, the newspaper a part of their history. He had worked up through the ranks and taken over as editor when his father retired, and it was expected his son would do the same.

"Hi Mike, it's Carrie. I just wanted to check in and let you know I've arrived at the hotel. Thanks for booking such a great place!"

"Thank Marcia for that," he replied, referring to his personal assistant. "I just told her to make sure it was close to the palace and had a desk that you could work at."

Typical Mike: Big time editor who ends his sentences with prepositions. She laughed at the thought. He would probably blow a gasket when he discovered the tab for her stay. She'd better make sure the article she would be writing after the press conference was worth it. She also made a mental note to thank Marcia when she got back; no doubt the woman had put a great deal of research into making Carrie's first international trip a memorable and enjoyable one.

"Have you read through the additional information I sent you?"

"Not yet, I just arrived this second. I'll make sure I check it all soon."

"You do that. Good luck with the conference tomorrow." With that, Mike disconnected.

Would it hurt the man to be just a bit more personable with his employees? You know, maybe asking how you're doing or did you get mugged in the airport or anything?

Carrie flicked through the welcome packet on the desk. She was pleased to discover there was 24/7 room service, and her package already included it at no extra cost if she substituted it for breakfast or dinner in one of their restaurants. She didn't feel like dressing for dinner tonight, and she had an idea that the required dress code to eat here would be of quite a high standard. She wasn't sure she had brought anything suitable, thinking only of the business meetings she would be attending and the fact that it was early August, when the temperatures were at their highest in Madrid.

Anyway, eating dinner alone in a fancy restaurant didn't feel quite right to her; it might be a little lonely and more than a little awkward. She would rather relax in smaller, more informal cafés than in elegant dining areas if she could, and if she couldn't, she would use the room service. Unless, of course, she found another journalist willing to share the experience with her; there must be other females alone on assignment here.

Carrie was also pleased to discover there was a laundry service, with a twice a day collection. That reminded her, she had better unpack. She hurried to unzip her case, hoping the afternoon heat and humidity would help remove the wrinkles the trip had made in her clothing. As she opened the wardrobe, she found she didn't need to worry. Rather than a trouser press, the wardrobe contained an upright steamer with a hanging rack. *At least I won't have to attend an audience with the prince in filthy rags,* she laughed to herself as she carefully hung up her garments. Steaming out the wrinkles could wait. Right now, her body longed for a long soak in that luxurious tub with the refreshing body salts she spotted decorating the shelf.

An hour later, Carrie emerged from the bathroom encased in the deliciously fluffy robe and slippers, feeling soothed and luxuriant. She giggled to herself, shocked at being so decadent in the middle of the afternoon during the workweek. She packed the clothing she had worn on the trip into one of the laundry bags, then walked to the door, opening it a tiny crack. Peeping up and down the hall, she saw there was no one in sight so she darted out just far enough in her robe to lay the bag in the hall and duck back into the privacy of her room, feeling like a naughty child who had just gotten away with something. Grabbing her laptop that had been charging while she bathed, she snuggled on the puffy, comfortable sofa to see what Mike had sent her.

The journalism profession had really changed with the advent of the internet. No more cables and telexes to stay in contact with your editor. Now all the research she needed to do was at her fingertips, reminding her how very much she respected journalists of years gone by for doing excellent work without the benefit of today's conveniences.

Thoughts like this always reminded Carrie of her mother, who had been studying journalism herself when she met Carrie's dad. Carrie smiled as she thought of the blossoming love affair, how her dad always said he'd swept her mom off her feet and dazzled her with his charm. *Oh, how I miss that man!*

Carrie smiled with pride at the thought of being the first-born child of such a beautiful couple. She wondered if she could ever find such a perfect partnership with a man. And if she did, would she follow in her mother's footsteps and choose motherhood as her career or try, as so many women do today, even in her Mormon faith, to balance career and motherhood?

Excuse me, but tonight's walk down Memory Lane is over. Mike's emails? Remember?

The first email contained a link to an in-depth article regarding Lonesome George. Lonesome George represented all that was at risk in the story of the oil spill that Carrie had been covering. In fact, this 100-year-old giant Pinta Island tortoise, the very last of his species, had become the 'poster boy' for conservationists around the world demanding action. Lonesome George was probably the most famous inhabitant of the Galapagos

Islands that lay right in the path of the Spanish oil spill. The press conference she would attend at the palace was to address action to clean up the spill and save the animals.

The story itself involved an environmental incident— a tanker owned by the Spanish Government, the Trayson Bay, had run aground near the shoreline of a major tourist resort on the stunning Ecuadorian coastline. The Spanish government had acted immediately, mobilizing cleanup units to handle the resultant oil spill. Other countries also rallied round, sending teams and equipment to assist with the major operation, attempting to prevent the massive ecological damage that such a disaster could cause.

Many newspapers, particularly the British rags, had been slamming Spain for the incident, crying out for a full independent inquiry into the cause of the accident. Carrie knew that the relationship between Great Britain and Spain was not in a great place at the moment. Certain referendums held in Britain had caused outrage within the Spanish government. In addition, Great Britain had been making noises about removing itself from the European Union, tired of the regulations enforced upon it by Brussels, not to mention being continually expected to financially bail out other floundering countries also in the Union.

As a journalist covering the international desk, Carrie had been following these stories carefully, aware that it was like a gently rumbling volcano, ready to explode at any time. It was her job to keep up with world news, and since Britain and the U.S. had a long history of alliance against threats, Britain had significance in some small way to the wellbeing of her own country.

At this point in time, Carrie had felt Britain was being unfair to Spain. She believed the Spanish government had been doing all they could under the unfortunate circumstances, quickly reacting to the spill, gladly accepting the help of any country willing to become involved, taking advice from teams more experienced with this kind of disaster, as well as launching an inquiry into the nature of the accident itself. As such, her published articles to date had been sympathetic and understanding to the Spanish government.

As a parliamentary monarchy, the current head of the Spanish royal family acted as both head of state and prime minister. So when a formal press conference held at the royal palace in Madrid had been announced to address the issues, her editor had jumped at the chance to send someone along not only to cover the conference, but to delve deeper into the government's actions, determining if they were really doing all they claimed.

Carrie had been over the moon to have been given the honor of attending, especially considering she had been covering the events from the beginning. This was an important assignment, possibly more suited to a more experienced reporter. Now Carrie had been given the chance and she was determined to rock and roll with it, hoping to win Mike's approval and make her family proud, particularly her mom back home.

The events had escalated to a state of panic within the conservation community, and indeed the world, considering the historic and ecological value of animals such as Lonesome George. The spill had yet to be contained and was fast heading toward the Galapagos Islands, an archipelago of volcanic islands in the Pacific Ocean situated on either side of the equator, just off the coast of Ecuador. The islands were one of the most important and diverse nature and marine reserves on the entire planet. If the spill contaminated the creatures there, it would be more than a disaster; it would be an utter tragedy. The very thought brought tears to Carrie's eyes.

Carrie could see why this article had such a poignant resonance with the current events and created such a disturbance among conservationists and animal lovers alike. The thought of yet another entire race, or perhaps several races, of God's creatures wiped off the face of His planet, this time due to a manmade disaster, should be more than enough to spur action from anyone not yet involved in the noble cause. Changing her position to sit yoga-style, cross-legged on the sofa, Carrie placed her laptop on the coffee table and pulled it toward her, opening a new document, and began to write.

It was only as she hit 'send' on her latest article about Lonesome George and the disaster that Carrie realized the natural light of the room had begun to fade and night was falling, being replaced by vibrant city lights. She checked the time on her laptop. It was almost 9 p.m. She knew from her quick read regarding Spanish culture that it was normal to eat dinner around ten at night, but she was ravenous! She pushed the coffee table back and uncrossed her legs, stretching them out and waggling her feet in an attempt to get the blood flowing back through them.

The story of Lonesome George had really touched her heart, and she had been so engrossed in writing the article she hadn't noticed the hours passing by. Standing up, she swiveled at the waist, freeing up her stiff back. With a reminder to herself to work at the desk next time like a sensible person, she wandered over to peruse the room service menu for options for tonight's meal.

Flipping through it, Carrie noted that she was in time to choose something from the all-day dining section. She was surprised to see the menu actually included very healthy foods—unusual for room service offerings in her limited experience traveling for business. In the end, she opted for a Caesar salad with grilled prawns and tiny slivers of bacon, adding a side order of steamed vegetables and a soda, although a burger and fries sure sounded tempting. It seemed to have been days since she last ate; the small tray served on the plane hardly counted as a decent meal.

After placing the order, she went to the wardrobe and found the one casual outfit she had packed. Just in case she might end up climbing over rocks to reach some oil-stricken bird in Ecuador, she had packed one pair of straight-legged denim jeans, sneakers, and a three-quarter sleeve t-shirt. She dressed quickly, slipping her feet back into the soft white slippers provided by the hotel. She knew the robe covered her from head to foot, but she couldn't very well answer the knock at the door and invite someone into her room wearing just that!

Hush now, Stomach! I'll feed you as soon as the food arrives.

As she impatiently waited for the knock on the door, she flipped through the movie guide to see what was showing, discarding some movies as too violent, too scary, or already seen too many times. She immediately skipped over those rated R and settled on a modern romance, which was in Spanish with English subtitles.

She loved a good romance where the heroine was a strong, independent woman who ended up swept off her feet by a modern-day knight in shining armor. *If only movies were more like real life, perhaps I'd be more inclined to think it really could happen for me one day*, she thought, being so engrossed in the unlikely tale on the screen that the knock at the door startled her. The call, "Room service, Ma'am" helped to settle her pounding heart. She opened the door and a waiter pushed in a cart and transferred a tray of covered plates and colorful flowers to the coffee table.

"Disfrute de su comida, Señorita," the service waiter said, disappearing as abruptly as had the bellhop earlier, neither giving her time to answer nor offer a small gratuity. Her stomach grumbled and she automatically placed a hand on it in embarrassment, even though she was alone in the room.

"Stop belly-aching!" she told her noisy stomach out loud, chuckling at the joke. She had a great sense of humor, but didn't consider herself 'funny.' She couldn't even remember a joke for ten minutes.

Lowering her head and closing her eyes, she gave thanks for the food she was about to eat, and for the opportunities she had been presented in her life. Finishing her prayer, she tucked in the lovely white linen napkin around her lap, finally sating her complaining tummy.

After she had tidied up, placed the used items back on the cart, and rolled it into the hallway for collection, Carrie decided she had better think about getting some sleep. She had a really important day tomorrow, and although she had prepared non-stop for this press conference since the day Mike told her that she was attending, last-minute checks would not go amiss. Undressing and wrapping herself back in the luxurious robe, she curled up on the bed to watch the end of the movie before falling into a deep, untroubled sleep.

Janice Limb Myers

CHAPTER THREE

Carrie stood, trying to decide what to wear. She had been up since the break of dawn going over her schedule, her prepared questions, checking the batteries in her recording device, packing her briefcase with everything she thought a young reporter might need to get the scoop of the century. She was now in a quandary over her final preparations. It was the height of summer, the temperatures in Madrid easily reaching between 100 and 110 degrees, with high humidity that leaves one feeling clammy and uncomfortable.

Taking that into consideration, her cream linen shift dress with matching bolero jacket was perfect, smart, yet not too oppressive for a summer's mid-morning meeting. However, the conference was at the royal palace. She wondered if that made a huge difference in her attire and chastised herself for not researching proper palace attire before the trip.

In the end, she decided it didn't matter. The palace was open to guided, ticketed tours and so would be subjected to a flood of tourists on a daily basis, all in various forms of attire. Her outfits were modest and appropriate for a business meeting back in New York

City, so they should be good enough for Madrid, royal palace or not.

Dressing in the shift, which came down to mid-calf, she checked in the mirror to ensure it was wrinkle-free. She paired it with expensive flat sandals, her best gold watch, and a small, simple gold pendant, which was the perfect length to be shown off by the gentle scoop of the neckline. Adding the bolero jacket, she decided the outfit was perfect. She had read that shoes and watches were particular status symbols in Spain, and wearing something less than classy would instantly brand you as a tourist, not worthy of service and attention except from pickpockets that roamed the great city; just another of the foibles of this strange culture that held so firm to its ancient traditions.

Satisfied with her mirrored reflection, Carrie gathered her briefcase and headed down for breakfast, looking forward to the experience of being under the stunning dome ceiling she had glimpsed the night before. She was sipping her orange juice and trying to control the nerves that were starting to set in as the full force of what she was about to do today hit her. She was about to meet a prince—a real, live prince!

Not only was Antonio Francisco Javier Carlos Dominguez a prince, he was the heir apparent, set to take over from his father within the next year as king of

Spain. Carrie had to get a grip on her emotions; this was not one of the Disney fairy tales she had loved so much as a child. She was twenty-seven years old and here to do a serious job. It wasn't as if she would be personally introduced to the prince or singled out in any way. She'd just be in a room with many other journalists and reporters, listening to him talk.

At best, she would be chosen to ask a direct question, and that was as far as her interaction would go. She didn't think she was normally such a dreamer, but this whole royalty thing had her just a little star-struck. She would be fine once she saw the man and confirmed that he was just an average person who put his pants on one leg at a time, just like everyone else, a man with normal problems and worries.

It was time to go. Although the palace was only a short walk away, Carrie knew that she would arrive looking like a wrung-out dishrag if she walked in the heat and humidity, so she used the international roaming on her cell phone to call the car company. She was pleased to see the familiar face of Miguel step into the lobby looking for her.

"Good morning," he beamed as she approached and escorted her to the same car as the day before, even carrying her briefcase for her.

Once she settled in the backseat with Miguel behind the wheel, she told him her destination.

"Ah yes, the press conference is today, I remember."

Miguel chatted as he drove the short distance, explaining that the palace was completed in 1764 in a neo-classical style. "It rose from the ashes of a Moorish castle, like a phoenix," he told her proudly, "when the Spanish defeated them and reclaimed our country. I am afraid this is as far as I can take the car, but I can escort you across the plaza."

The car came to a halt and Carrie exited, getting her first glimpse of the sprawling white building behind the wrought iron and gold gates. It was more like an extremely large, highly decorated stately home than a Disney castle, but it was beautiful just the same. Due to the size of the palace, there were several entrances, and Carrie was glad that the car company had obviously received a copy of her schedule from the ever-efficient Marcia back at the newspaper office and knew exactly where to take her. She and Miguel strolled across the plaza together, taking in the amazing sight before them. Carrie needed to show her press card as she reached the entrance, and Miguel showed his I.D. card, talking to the guard in rapid Spanish.

Guards were dotted around and several young, smartly-dressed Spanish women were waiting to greet the arriving journalists and escort them to the conference. One of the girls approached them with an efficient smile, rattling off her greeting. She directed her words to Miguel and practically ignored Carrie. He spoke sharply back to her, and the woman gave a small nod of apology, turning to Carrie and indicating that she should follow her. Carrie had no clue what was going on; her smattering of Spanish was not nearly enough to cope with the depth or the speed of the conversation, although she surmised this young woman had assumed Miguel to be the correspondent and Carrie his aid.

"This is where I must leave you. The press conference is to be held in the imperial hall, and only your identification as a member of the press will get you further into the palace today," Miguel informed her. "Do not look so lost, Señorita Carpenter; the conference will be held in English." His eyes were laughing at her as he spoke, but in a friendly, understanding way. He held out her briefcase for her. "Please follow the Señorita and she will show you the way."

The girl was waiting impatiently, so Carrie hurriedly took her leave, trotting after her hostess across the marble floor. Boy was she glad she hadn't worn heels! She was ushered through the long, wide corridors to the room where the conference was being held. Reaching the entrance, the girl disappeared and Carrie was face-to-face with an armed guard. She held out her press card again and the man nodded and raised the red velvet rope that was barring the door.

Entering the room, Carrie could see only rows and rows of chairs laid out in the center of the great hall. They were sectioned into blocks, ten across and ten back, eight blocks in all. Wow, they were certainly prepared for a very large turnout! The room was still quite empty with only a few of the seats taken. She chose a seat near the center of the room in the second row to avoid being directly in the front. Settling down, she opened her briefcase to go over her notes, hoping to settle her nerves.

"Gosh, you're brave," said a plummy voice as a woman took the chair on Carrie's right.

Carrie glanced up from her reading and saw a more mature lady with short salt and pepper hair, wearing a dark navy suit and a white blouse with a high, lacy collar. Her outfit was finished off with a string of pearls at her neck and sensible lace-up shoes on her feet.

"Edith Summers, *The London Enquirer*," she introduced, holding out her hand and giving Carrie a firm, no-nonsense handshake.

"Carrie Carpenter, *The Daily New Yorker*. And why am I brave?"

"Ah, an American, explains it a bit. The outfit, girly. Bucking the trend a bit there, aren't we?"

Carrie's face fell. "What's wrong with it?"

"Oh nothing, it's just the Spanish are terribly traditional, always dark suits for business meetings. Silly really—you go to a hospital and the doctors are wearing jeans and t-shirts. Same in the post office, town hall, wherever. You go into local shops and the girls are in shorts and strappy tops, but the slightest sniff of authority, such as notaries or banks, and it has to be dark suits, no matter what the weather. Jolly inconvenient!"

Carrie looked around, seeing that the room had filled up considerably since her arrival. True enough, male and female alike were all dressed in various shades of dark clothing, from slate grey to black. "Oh dear, I didn't know." *I'm surprised Marcia didn't include this traditional dress in her instructions.*

"Not to worry, I expect they'll be used to it, considering this place is open to tourists; they must see some sights," the woman snorted, her loud laugh braying across the room. "Funny lot anyway, take a bit of getting used to, they do. How are you finding them?"

"Friendly for the most part, but with a habit of disappearing on you," Carrie laughed and the woman laughed with her.

"Yes, comes across as quite rude, but it's just their way to walk away in the middle of a conversation, hang up the phone without saying goodbye, that sort of thing. They think we Brits are ridiculous with our 'pleases' and 'thank yous' all the time, bit of a joke to them. Still, you might fare a bit better, being a New Yorker. Aren't you all supposed to be a bit abrupt?"

"Well, I guess some are and some aren't. Like every other place in the world, there are nice people and some not so nice, but I'm not a native."

"Oh, here we go." She nodded toward the podium.

There was no time to continue the conversation as rows of guards filed in, taking up their positions all the way up each side and along the back of the room. *Talk about a Disney fairy tale! I'm right in the middle of one! Wow, those uniforms!* As Carrie looked around, she saw every seat filled, as well as some people standing at the back. She was glad this oil spill tragedy attracted so much attention; the more press it got, the more help would be offered. Conservationists worldwide were demanding action, and from all the press in attendance, it appeared the palace had heard their demands.

"Ladies and gentlemen," the man who had just taken the stage with great pomp and ceremony began, "it is my honor to introduce your host, the Crown Prince Antonio Francisco Javier Carlos Dominguez." Carrie had expected the prince to be wearing some regalia for the occasion, but the man who stepped up to the podium was dressed demurely in a dark grey suit with a lighter grey silk tie. *Susan was right. I've seen too many fairy tales.*

"Now comes the main event," Edith leaned over to whisper in Carrie's ear.

Like most Spaniards, the prince wasn't overly tall, but he was taller than many she had seen, standing at about 5 foot 10 inches, she supposed. As did the others, he moved with that quiet, understated grace, a flair and style in mannerisms that Carrie had never seen before in anyone but trained dancers.

As he turned to face his audience, Carrie gasped. He was incredibly handsome, his masculine features highlighted by eyes as dark as the richest chocolate, topped by ebony-black hair that was swept back from his high brow. His look was intense, and for a few seconds, it seemed to fall directly on Carrie, burning its way into her, as if he could see right into her very soul. Or was she just being starry-eyed again?

When the fleeting moment passed, Carrie could breathe again. She missed the introduction, as she was too busy trying to figure out what had just happened. As he'd looked at her, she had felt her heart jolt. It was as though someone had given her an electric shock. Then it had raced in response to the unfamiliar feeling, and she had felt her cheeks flush.

"He has that effect on everybody; he's quite the hunk, isn't he?" Edith hissed in her ear. "Wouldn't mind a private audience after this 'presser' with him myself." She raised a suggestive eyebrow at Carrie, who blushed furiously in response to the inappropriate comment, as well as with the realization that her unwarranted response to the prince had been obvious enough for Edith to notice. Had the prince noticed as well? *Oh, how embarrassing, Carrie! You're making an idiot of yourself already!*

Pulling herself together, she got her head back into business, listening intently to the statements and the subsequent questions being asked and answered. The four-hour presser went by in a blur of information and ended with a heartfelt plea from the prince on behalf of all of Spain for as much assistance as possible. He begged other countries not to sit back and watch the horror unfold, but to get involved in the cleanup and spill containment before it was too late to save the wildlife. This was an event of great magnitude to the entire world, not just to Spain.

Interviewers called out more questions to the prince, but he stood regally, informing them that he was very sorry, but he had a meeting with a group of ecologists who specialized in the Galapagos Islands. They would supply him with detailed information on upcoming tide projections and how they would affect the current position of the shifting oil spill. The entire audience broke into rapturous applause as the meeting came to a close. They gathered their belongings and dashed toward the doors, hoping to be the first to get their copy written and sent back to their waiting editors.

"You can certainly tell he has been in training for this all his life, can't you?" Edith asked Carrie as she packed away her recorder and notebook. "Diplomatic to a T, and incredibly well-versed in world politics. He's going to make an excellent king."

Carrie had to agree with her, as she couldn't fault how professional the prince had been. He had achieved the perfect balance of ceremony and information, and had also established a connection with the people. She admired how he had given the facts sincerely and honestly, making no excuses or attempts to sugarcoat the scale of the disaster. He had delivered his request for assistance with just the right amount of emotion to show he cared deeply about the consequences but would stay strong in the face of adversity. He surely was going to make an excellent king, just as Edith had suggested.

As Carrie turned to leave, she noticed that most of the reporters had not been permitted to leave and were still crowded around the door. She wondered what on earth could be going on, but her question was soon answered as the man who had opened the presser stepped back up to the podium.

"If I may have your attention, please. Don Antonio sincerely regrets his hasty departure due to a previously arranged meeting. He is aware that some of you still had questions, and the opportunity was not given. Therefore, those who were scheduled to ask questions but did not have their topics covered in the conference are requested to attend a formal dinner tonight here at the palace, where our discussions can be continued. The invitation is extended to the following…."

As the names of the people and their corresponding newspapers and TV channels were read out, Carrie was stunned to hear her name called. She had submitted her specific questions to Mike for approval, and he must have then submitted them to the palace. She was still quite new to all this, and had no idea so much went on behind the scenes to set these things up. She had thought the questions and answers were random, but apparently, not all of them were.

"Lucky thing!" Edith exclaimed, as grumblings echoed around the room from those not included in the invitation. "I wouldn't have complained about being in his company for another few hours."

She nudged Carrie with a knowing look. *This woman is completely outrageous*, Carrie thought, but it was nice to have another female to talk with.

"What should I wear, Edith?" she asked, gnawing at her bottom lip. "I've already gotten it wrong once."

Edith looked thoughtful. "Hmmm, well he said 'formal dinner,' and that to me would say a white tie event—you know, short jackets, sashes, and military and civil regalia for the men, evening gowns, tiaras, and elbow-length gloves for the ladies."

Carrie gulped; she didn't have anything even remotely suitable among the items she had brought with her.

"Let me go and check," Edith declared, marching fearlessly up to the master of ceremonies that had hosted the event, joining him on stage while being watched closely by armed guards. She chatted easily with the man, her braying laugh heard again across the emptying room, as the reporters were now allowed to leave. Carrie watched as Edith removed her notebook from her briefcase and the man wrote something down. With a smile and a brisk handshake that stunned the man, she returned to her seat next to Carrie.

"Yes, white tie tonight. The full details have been emailed to the editors, so I expect yours will get in touch soon. I take it you don't have anything suitable since you wouldn't have been expecting this?"

"Not even close," Carrie groaned. *Unless, of course, it would be okay to show up in a t-shirt and jeans? Probably not!*

"Typical royalty though, eh? Just expect everyone to have appropriate items at the drop of a hat. Never mind, we are in Madrid and I have a plan." She glanced at her watch. "It's three o'clock now; the shops will be closed for the siesta. Why don't we head back to our hotels, grab a spot of room service lunch while we write up our articles, then I'll meet you at six when the shops will be open again. Sergio gave me the names of a few places that should be able to fit you out quickly. You don't need to be back here 'til nine, so three hours ought to do it. What do you say, up for a shopping trip in one of the most stylish cities in the world?"

"Sure am," Carrie responded emphatically. "Thanks, Edith. You're a lifesaver."

"No problem. Let's just make sure we exchange email addresses; I want the scoop on the night, and not about the oil spill! I'm flying home first thing in the morning, so I won't see you again; I'll be dying to know how it went and what he's like in a less restricted environment. Promise?"

"Absolutely. Let's do that right now."

The two women exchanged their contact details and parted ways. Carrie was surprised to find Miguel waiting for her in the lobby; she had intended just walking back to the hotel, but she was glad of the quick trip, as she was eager to get to work. She told Miguel about the invitation and the shopping trip, conversation now easier between them as she was beginning to understand the Spanish accent. He insisted on picking her up and driving her to the shops. He claimed she wouldn't have time to make her way back to the hotel but would have to go straight to the palace, and she couldn't very well walk or take a taxi in her new gown. She had laughingly accepted his kind offer—the vision of her parading the streets of Madrid in a full-length evening gown amused her greatly. She would just have to make sure she got enough insider information from the prince to keep her boss from complaining about the shopping trip and the driver's bill.

Back in her room, Carrie settled down at the desk and opened her email. She laughed as she read the communication from her editor: *Hear you've been invited to some fancy schmancy dinner. Be at the palace at 9 p.m., evening gown and all that jazz. Put it on expenses, but make sure it's worth it—get all the details you can, especially about the investigation into the accident. Expect your copy from today soon, Mike.*

The next email was from Marcia, who had written to give Carrie more details on the event and the required dress code. She had obviously been researching it online, as the information she provided was highly detailed and included the names and addresses of shops she felt would provide her with an appropriate outfit.

Carrie felt Marcia's list might be more useful than Edith's simply because she knew her better than Edith did. She had a feeling that the older woman would attempt to steer Carrie to the highest fashion boutiques and to the more revealing couture preferred by current designers, which Carrie would consider entirely inappropriate in any setting. This way, they could compare lists, knowing Marcia would have looked into the price ranges more thoroughly for Carrie's sake. *Thank goodness for Marcia!* Feeling more positive about things, Carrie got down to work.

CHAPTER FOUR

Carrie stared at herself in the dressing room mirror, unable to believe her eyes. She and Edith compared the lists they had been given, but in the end, Miguel was the one who selected the store from the names they had discussed. He then escorted the ladies inside and explained to the assistant in Spanish that Carrie needed a full outfit for a formal dinner at the palace.

As designer dresses had been shown to her one after the other by two attentive assistants, Carrie had pulled the patient Miguel aside, explaining to him that she was a Mormon and would require something more modest than the strapless, cleavage-showing, figure-hugging creations being presented to her.

"I do not understand this word, Mormon," he had said to her, a confused expression on his face.

"It's my religion," she explained. "I belong to The Church of Jesus Christ of Latter-day Saints. People refer to us as 'Mormons.' I don't believe it's appropriate to put my body on display as much as this," she said, indicating the dresses the assistants were holding out for her perusal.

"Ah, religion, I understand, although I am not familiar with the name. You require something more modest, yes?"

"Yes, thank you," Carrie said, relieved at the approval she saw in his countenance. She hadn't noticed Edith walking over to them.

"Oh, a Mormon. So sorry, Carrie, I didn't realize. You must think me terrible with all my comments earlier." Edith pealed with laughter ending in a bit of a snicker.

"Not at all," Carrie replied. "It's not for me to judge others in that way, and besides, none of us can help our thoughts sometimes!"

"I'm surprised you haven't heard of it, Miguel," Edith scolded. "There is a temple here in Madrid, up on the hill, not very far from the airport."

Miguel thought for a second, and then realization dawned on him. "Ah, of course, Templo de Mormón. I am sorry, the American pronunciation confused me. Of course I know this Templo well and have delivered many passengers there."

Miguel left to explain the situation to the two women, who nodded their agreement. One woman led Carrie to a changing room and handed her an ice-blue silk creation. She slipped it on and couldn't believe the reflection in the mirror was really her. The dress had an intricate silk-lined lace panel that covered her cleavage and upper arms and was fitted across the bust and to the waist, where it flared out into a full, floor-length skirt. A narrow, powder blue sash encircled the waist, connecting at the back to drape down over the skirt at the rear.

The ice-blue color highlighted the darker blue of her eyes, making them sparkle more brightly than they ever had before. Her blond hair looked richer against the flattering color. As she was admiring the dress, the sales assistant stepped into the dressing room. She turned Carrie around and critically examined every inch of the dress. She tugged a little here and a little there to adjust the way the dress hung.

"You like?" she asked in broken English.

"Yes," Carrie breathed. "Very much. I feel like Cinderella going to the ball!"

"Bien. Bien."

The girl disappeared, but soon both women returned laden with boxes. They began to open the boxes, sending reams of tissue paper flying around the dressing room as they pulled out purses and shoes. They compared the shades of blue to the dress and contrasting sash. Finally, they were content with their selections and presented Carrie with a pair of matching strappy heels accented by discreetly placed crystals here and there to add glamour, and a matching clutch purse.

Adding the white, elbow-length gloves to the outfit, Carrie looked at herself and saw one of the princesses from her beloved fairy tales from her childhood. She twirled delightedly, reveling in the beauty of the dress. She carefully guarded herself from too much vanity, preferring to admire only the skill of the designer and the exquisite fabric and cut.

Normally, she wouldn't even consider spending this amount of money on a whole wardrobe, never mind a single outfit. She had to remind herself that this was a requirement, not an option. This was necessary for her job and the call to arms she hoped to raise through her articles. She knew that no country in the world was as experienced at dealing with oil spills as America. The natural world needed the U.S. and its resources right now, and she would do everything she could to get them involved. She had to admit, wearing this for an evening was not that much of a hardship! *At least I'll get to do my job in style tonight!*

As she stepped from the dressing room back into the shop, Edith's eyes filled with tears. "You look so beautiful, Carrie," she sniffed. "You remind me of my daughter at her debutante ball."

"Thank you so much, Edith; it's all because of you. I feel like a princess in a Disney movie right now."

With Edith's words, Carrie now understood why Edith was so relaxed in the presence of royalty. She knew the required traditions and had no fear in approaching the man earlier. For her daughter to have her own coming-of-age ball, she must have been a debutante, and that made them a high society family back in the UK. She was probably used to being in the company of influential people. It made Carrie wonder why Edith was even here working as a journalist. It was a question for another time. *I hope I can learn to be as relaxed as Edith.*

Carrie realized the two women were whispering to Miguel, gesturing toward Carrie. "The girls, they say your outfit is perfect, but your hair it is not suitable," he translated for her.

Carrie instinctively touched her locks. After the shower she took after sending in her article to Mike, she had left her hair loose, simply drying it quickly with the blow drier provided by the hotel. It now tumbled in loose waves down her back and around the sides of her face. The women were gesturing that it needed to be in an up-do to be appropriate. One of them guided Carrie to a seat and pressed her down firmly, talking to her in Spanish all the while.

"She says she's calling her sister, who is a hair dresser. She says her sister will complete the look you need for this particular occasion." *Thank goodness Miguel decided to stay and translate for me.*

While Carrie waited, Edith instructed her on some points of etiquette she would need to know, one of which was to remove her watch. For some reason, despite watches being a status symbol, they were not permitted at white tie events. Even Edith didn't know why it was the case, but she suspected it might be that glancing at it, even accidently, would appear rude to the hosts.

Soon a woman arrived at the boutique laden with bags and cases, two small children in tow. Carrie's heart ached as she looked at the children, one boy and one girl, both of whom Carrie was sure were no older than nine. They were adorable with their olive skin and dark eyes. The little girl was wearing a dress that could easily put the designer creations in the shop to shame, and she looked so cute in it. Her dark hair was in ringlets, each side tied with a bow matching the red sash on her white dress. The boy was more casually dressed, wearing cargo shorts and a polo shirt, but was equally as adorable as his sister.

"I'm sorry, I had to bring them with me," the woman apologized as she began to open bags and remove equipment. Carrie longed to talk to the children but wasn't sure if they would understand any English. She said hello in her minimal Spanish, and the little girl instantly started talking to her in her native language.

"Elena," her mother interrupted. "En Inglés, por favor."

The little girl suddenly became shy, hiding her face with her hands. Peeking out between her fingers, she hesitantly addressed Carrie. "Hello, I am Elena. Your dress, I like very much."

"Thank you; I was just thinking how pretty yours is too. Your English is very good!"

Pleased with the praise, Carrie and Elena chatted in a mix of bad, but understandable, Spanish and English, Elena's mother helping out when they were stuck. Miguel had taken the boy outside, presumably to look at and play in the car. By the time they returned, the conversation had moved away from dresses, and the boy ventured over to join in, asking questions about America in his broken English. Carrie was so enchanted with the children that she barely noticed what was happening with her hair and make-up.

"Finished!" the woman exclaimed, stepping back to scrutinize her efforts. The three women examined her as if she was an exhibit in an art gallery, finally nodding their approval. The little girl reached up and touched a tendril of Carrie's hair.

"This color, no see much in Spain, I like it for me."

"Your hair is beautiful as it is," Carrie replied, stroking the rich chestnut curls. "God gave you this color, which means it is perfect for you; nothing else would look as good."

The mother smiled at Carrie. "Come, let us look."

She led Carrie back to the dressing room, where she once again examined herself in the mirror, making faces at herself to believe the reflection staring back belonged to her. Her hair was piled on her head in a series of intricate twists, a few small, sparkling crystals peeping delicately through the design. One or two tendrils had been curled into loose, gentle ringlets to frame her face. The make-up was subtle, highlighting her delicate features in a barely-there manner, her clear complexion and sparkling eyes needing no assistance other than to let the natural beauty shine. *This woman has worked a miracle!* She couldn't thank everyone enough for all they had done to ensure she fit in at this occasion that was well beyond her normal comfort zone.

"No tears," the woman told her firmly. "You will ruin the look."

Carrie tried to offer to pay the woman for her work, but she waved the offer away. "It was my pleasure to help," she said, and Carrie understood that to press the matter would offend her. All she could do was thank them all again.

"It is time to go; I must take you to the palace now." Miguel stated.

Carrie nodded; the confidence previously gained by the sight of the dress in the mirror now fled as she realized the enormity of Miguel's simple statement. Yes, it was time to go.

She rolled down one white glove and removed her watch, popping it into her new purse. Edith had told her that if anyone older than her was either not wearing gloves, or removed theirs, she would need to remove hers as well. The last thing she wanted was to take off her gloves only to reveal her watch underneath! When the number of possibilities of what could go wrong during dinner hit her, she almost felt sick at the thought.

Seated in the back of the car, Carrie offered a silent prayer, asking for help to find the courage within herself to go through with this, and to handle it to the best of her ability so her actions would reflect well on her faith and show honor to God. She instantly felt calm, comforted by the certain knowledge that God would always listen to her fears, even if they did seem trivial, and walk by her side to assist her. In this case, she was confident in the fact that her desire to succeed wasn't a selfish one; it was born of a desire to do the greatest good within her power in the current situation.

She thanked Miguel and Edith for all their help and said a fond farewell to her new friend. As she walked toward the royal palace entrance, the two looked on like proud parents, pleased with how smoothly everything had gone and how beautiful Carrie looked.

The staff led Carrie into a formal hall that looked as if it doubled as an art gallery. There she found a gathering of well-dressed people, some standing in small groups and chatting in hushed tones. Others were milling about, taking in the art displayed on the walls. She thought she recognized quite a few faces but decided she must be mistaken.

Etiquette demanded she be escorted by a gentleman into the dining room. When a butler announced the members of the press should make their way through, a man who appeared to be in his mid to late thirties immediately approached her. He was tall and slender, with black hair greying slightly at the temples, giving him that distinguished salt-and-pepper look. He was handsome, but his Roman nose gave his already slender face an almost gaunt look, and Carrie could see a deep sadness in his eyes. Still, he was doing a good job of being charming and courteous, and Carrie was glad of the escort, saving her the embarrassment of having to request one.

"May I?" he enquired, offering his arm for Carrie to take as decorum demanded. She recognized the accent as a fellow American, feeling relieved that she wasn't the only one here.

"Pete Barker, *Economist Weekly*, based in Washington," he informed her.

"Carrie Carpenter. I wouldn't have thought the financial publications would have a major interest in this story. Surely it's of more interest to the political and human interest press?"

"Indeed, but believe me, an ecological disaster and how it's dealt with has a huge impact on international relations and subsequent trading. Not to mention the way the shares of the involved companies perform."

"I hadn't considered that aspect," Carrie said thoughtfully. She hoped she would be seated somewhere she could talk with him further. As a journalist, she still had a lot to learn; someone looking at the event from a completely different perspective could certainly broaden her views. She felt she was going to be in for a very interesting night.

Carrie got her wish; the man who had escorted her was seated to her left. The dining room was as opulent as the imperial hall had been, with the impossibly long table situated in the center of the room. Silverware and crystal the likes of which Carrie had never seen adorned it. Looking at her place setting, she counted twelve sets of cutlery. *Good grief! If I eat twelve courses, I won't fit into my dress by the end of the night—the seams would explode!*

Misinterpreting her worried look, Pete was quick to attempt to educate her. "Just start from the outside and work your way in, or wait for someone else to start and follow their lead," he hissed into her ear, hoping to help her out so she didn't embarrass herself.

"Thank you," Carrie said, being polite as ever, even though she had known that much at least. In fact, it was all the way back to her teenage years that her youth leaders at church had put on a series of etiquette classes for the girls, the culmination of which was a beautiful dinner to test their newly-acquired etiquette skills. The church's cultural hall had been transformed into a gorgeous Italian restaurant decorated in white, black and red. Men dressed in tuxedos served the meal, making the girls feel really special. Carrie couldn't remember which she loved more, the large brandy snifters on the tables filled with water and black mollies swimming in them or the dessert served over dry ice, creating smoke that encircled the frozen chocolate bon-bons, making it appear they were floating on air. Yes, they had learned as teenagers that when in doubt, just work the silverware from the outside in.

Carrie looked around the room, noting there seemed to be twenty-three reporters seated at the table. The men outnumbered the women greatly, but of the three women, she was relieved to see the other two also wore full-length ball gowns, although perhaps a touch more glamorous and definitely more revealing than hers. Neither of them were wearing gloves, and Carrie wondered if she had been steered wrong and should remove her gloves. She decided no, the Spanish women helped her put together the outfit, and if anyone should be familiar with the correct dress, it would be the people of this country.

The master of ceremonies stepped into the room, and Carrie watched with interest as he announced the arrival of various heads of state and politicians from other European countries. She had been right in thinking that she knew some of the faces. Obviously, this dinner was something that had been arranged previously as a meeting of political minds. The inclusion of the journalists from the conference must have been a last-minute decision made by the prince. Carrie wished she had been allowed to bring her notebook or her recorder as there were going to be many things discussed here tonight that Mike would be very glad to get his hands on. She was startled out of trying to memorize all the attendees by the next announcement.

"Ladies and Gentlemen, may I present to you the Crown Prince, Don Antonio." *Be still, my heart!*

The men rose at the announcement, but Carrie, watching the other women present, determined it wasn't appropriate for her to do so. She was able to stay seated and drink in the vision that entered the room. The prince was now in formal attire, a white bow tie around a starched white wing collar, an equally pristine white waistcoat beneath the black tailcoat jacket with peaked lapels. Slim gold epaulettes adorned the jacket, with gold trim at the cuffs and a regalia displayed on the left breast, though Carrie couldn't make out the symbols from this distance. She felt that same spark and flutter of excitement as she had experienced earlier when she had seen him for the first time.

He was so incredibly handsome, and now formally attired, just needed a stripe down his pants, knee-high boots, and a sword at his side to look just like a Disney prince brought to life.

Carrie almost giggled aloud at the thought but managed to keep herself in check. She noted that the few females in the group of politicians were also wearing gloves, and she watched as a butler hurried to the other two female journalists who were not gloved, handing them pairs similar to hers. The master of ceremonies waited patiently as they hurried to tug them on before making his next announcement.

"Ladies and Gentlemen, may I present to you King Benito and Queen Isabella."

Carrie gasped. She hadn't expected the king and queen to attend! She hurried to stand along with the rest of the room. She had wondered why the prince had made no attempt to sit down and had remained standing behind his chair, looking straight ahead and not making eye contact with anyone. She wished Edith were invited to the event; she would have ensured Carrie kept her feet on the ground!

Once the king and queen were settled, the prince took his seat and the rest of the room followed. Carrie realized with a blush that she was one of the last, having taken time to arrange her full skirt before she sat, and everyone was watching her. She kept her gaze on the settings before her, careful not to catch anyone's eye. As the king and queen formally welcomed them, butlers seemed to appear from everywhere, each taking a section of the table, distributing wine from crystal carafes into one of the many glasses placed at each setting. Carrie quickly turned over her wine glass just as the waiter leaned to fill it.

"I'm sorry, I don't drink alcohol. May I please just have water?" she asked timidly. The waiter hesitated for only a fraction of a second before clicking his fingers high in the air. An under-butler hurried to his side, and on receiving instructions, he smiled at Carrie and removed the array of various-sized crystal glasses from her setting, placing them all on a silver tray. He disappeared and returned with a large crystal glass and a crystal decanter of water. He placed the glass beside her and filled it, leaving the decanter on the table in front of her place setting. Carrie thanked him, and as she looked up and glanced around the room, she was disconcerted to find the prince watching her, a curious expression on his face. She flushed under his gaze and quickly looked away, turning to Pete to involve herself in a work-related conversation regarding the economic impact of the oil disaster.

Carrie was pleased when the food was blessed before the meal, and the rest of the dinner went smoothly. As each course was served, Carrie began to relax into the occasion. Different wines accompanied each course, but the butler bypassed Carrie each time, only laying down his carafe or decanter to refill her water when necessary. She had been concerned about the food, but she was relieved to find that the Spanish did not eat many meat dishes, preferring fresh salads, vegetables, and seafood.

The only heavy meat dish was of pork, which Carrie enjoyed. Each course was of small portions, and she found herself able to keep up after all. Even the final dessert course was fresh strawberries served with a side pastry that looked like it would be sickly sweet, but on tasting it, she found it was actually quite plain. It felt a little strange eating with gloves on, but the queen had kept hers on so Carrie did the same.

The conversation had been very interesting, concentrating mainly on what the prince had learned from the ecologists earlier in the day and what steps could be taken to counteract the movement of the spill by the tides. Each country represented was willing to give whatever assistance they could, whether it was expertise, equipment, or financial assistance.

At that moment, Carrie was so proud of the human race, how they could unite this way and come together to find a solution to a problem with no blame or recrimination. How she wished it would always be that way, all across the world—people working in harmony to care for and protect what mattered to them, without requiring a disaster to bond them.

She was well able to hold her own in any of the conversations that had gone on around her, and a few times, she had caught the prince watching her section of the table intently, as if listening in. However, Edith had told her only to address people as far as two people either side, and perhaps the same directly across from her if the size of the table allowed it, so she had no opportunity to hear the prince's opinions on their discussions.

Mostly, though, the journalists listened keenly to what was going on with the politicians at the other end of the table. As was probably fitting for a society table setting, they were farthest away from the members of the royal family, and discussions only broke out when someone said something controversial or particularly important. Her dinner companion, Pete Barker, had a keen mind, and Carrie enjoyed his company for the short times that discussions were possible throughout the meal.

Once the butlers cleared the final course, coffee was served. Carrie had been too engrossed in a conversation at the other end of the table to notice the cup placed in front of her. Once she noticed it, she simply ignored it, still sipping on her water. The cups were small, and Carrie could tell by the smell that the coffee was strong. She pushed the cup back a fraction, away from under her nose. Pete raised an eyebrow at her but made no comment. They continued to listen to a particularly interesting conversation, and when it was over, the top end of the table became silent.

Draining his cup, Pete turned to address her. "I take it you don't drink coffee?"

"No, I don't. I'm a Mormon, and we don't drink coffee or strong drinks."

"Oh, how interesting! Mind if we swap, then? I love the stuff, but I'm more used to a Grande from Starbucks than these tiny cups."

"Feel free," Carrie laughed as he deftly switched his empty cup and saucer for her full one.

"You never told me which newspaper you worked for," he said as he sipped at his second coffee.

"Oh, I'm sorry; there's been so little opportunity to talk. I'm Carrie Carpenter, *The Daily New Yorker.*"

He looked impressed at her response. "Good to meet you, Carrie. That's quite a highbrow paper you work for there. I wouldn't have thought they'd have been running the human-interest side of this?"

"Our readers are interested in all aspects, and I've been mostly concentrating on the environmental impact and the political implications, but aren't even the most intelligent of readers drawn to the human-interest side when it involves royalty?"

Pete laughed. "I guess you're right. Especially as it's the real royals that have been restored since the last one abdicated, you know, the one that was handpicked by Franco?"

"Juan Carlos, yes. There were quite a few scandals revolving around him, weren't there?"

"Not sure this lot will be any better. There are a few rumors that the good prince is a bit of a ladies' man. I think it'll be a sad day for the country when he takes over."

Carrie bristled at the unproven aspersions cast against the prince, but she had no time to respond as a loud clearing of a throat caught her attention. She looked up to the top end of the table, and she once again caught the prince watching her. His face was impassive, but his eyes burned with a strange light. Carrie was torn between the butterflies in her tummy as she looked at him and the feeling that perhaps she had offended her hosts by refusing the wine and coffee. Well, if he was offended, that was too bad. She would never condemn others for practices that she herself believed were wrong and accepted that people had different opinions, and she wasn't going to go against her beliefs for anyone, not even a prince!

She titled her chin defiantly, and thought she caught a flash of amusement cross his face. The moment was quickly gone, leaving Carrie wondering if she had really seen it. The king and queen chose that moment to retire from the occasion, and everyone stood as they took their leave. The politicians soon followed, everyone having pledged what they could and a plan of action now put in place.

Left alone with the journalists, the prince now moved several seats down the table, sitting among them.

"I trust you have had a pleasant and interesting evening?"

They all murmured their agreement, and one jumped in with a question, opening up the question and answer session. It was going well, and Carrie was getting some fantastic information for her articles until one journalist decided to push his luck and go off topic.

"Is it true that your father will retire this year, and you will take over the throne?"

"I cannot answer that question for you. That is a question you would have to ask the king."

"Come on, you must know?"

"That is a personal matter for him to discuss when he feels ready to do so."

Carrie could tell that the prince was growing agitated with this line of questioning, but he held his decorum and kept his tone level.

"What about the Swiss princess? Is there any truth to the rumors that you are to be wed?"

"Princess Nadine is a dear friend of mine. That is all I am willing to say on the matter."

Now Carrie was getting irritated with her fellow journalists. They had been given this amazing opportunity, and there they were at the prince's table taking advantage of it. If they persisted, they would ruin this for everyone. She told herself this was the only source of her annoyance and pushed down the slight flare of jealousy she felt at the mention of the prince being wed to another. She was as irritated with herself as she was with the others.

Jealously was not a becoming emotion, and one she'd tried to avoid all her life. She succumbed to it a number of times as a teenager but thought she had conquered the emotion. So why should it rear its ugly head now over this man? After all, she had only met him today and knew nothing about him except his public persona. It was time to turn this conversation back to where it was meant to be.

"Prince Antonio?" Carrie had to clear her throat and swallow hard before she could continue; saying his first name and addressing him directly had made her mouth go dry. "Can you tell us how the investigation into the cause of the accident is going, and a little about the agency that's conducting the investigation?"

He turned to face Carrie directly. The tiny smile was barely noticeable, but the relief and gratitude in his eyes were obvious.

"That's an excellent question."

He held her gaze as he spoke, and Carrie was mesmerized. She could hear her heart pounding in her ears and wondered if everyone else could hear it too. She had to concentrate hard to focus on his answer.

The prince proceeded to answer in detail, and Carrie was reassured that the country was indeed taking full responsibility and doing everything they could. Just as he concluded his answer, a man hurried in and whispered in his ear. Excusing himself from the table, the prince followed the man from the room. The journalists looked at each other, wondering what was going on. They began to chat among themselves, discussing the night's events. The room went silent as the prince returned, a smile on his face.

"Ladies and gentlemen of the press," he declared. "I am pleased to inform you that I have just had a call from the president of the United States. He has informed me that he has deployed three trained crews from Worldwide Disaster Cleanup, who will be arriving by military cargo plane tomorrow morning, along with all the equipment they can carry. Unfortunately, their specially-equipped ships would take too long to arrive, but we have assured him that any amount of Spanish naval ships will be made available to them, and he has indicated that the crews will be able to work with those almost as well as their own."

Carrie felt like cheering, and she and Pete turned to smile at each other. They both knew Worldwide Disaster Cleanup was a firm specializing in the handling of chemical disasters, and they were the best in the business. If anyone could coordinate the massive amounts of assistance into an organized and efficient cleanup operation to minimize environmental impact and possibly save the Galapagos Islands from contamination, it would be them.

People were already making moves to leave, and the prince laughed, dropping his perfect composure for once. "I can see you are anxious to get back to your laptops and report this news to the world. Therefore, I think that concludes our meeting for the night."

The prince departed once more and Pete was already standing, waiting to escort Carrie out.

"Isn't that great news! I knew our guys would come through," he said enthusiastically.

"It *is* great news," Carrie responded. She was proud of her country, and proud of all the people who had reported on this disaster, raising awareness of the seriousness of the matter. She felt that she had done her part to help, ensuring the American people were informed of the situation and how much it meant despite occurring so far away. She was about to take Pete's arm to walk out together when she noticed the under-butler who had served her the water hovering by her side.

"Excuse me, Miss, but the prince has requested your presence in the drawing room for a few moments."

Pete and Carrie glanced at each other and Pete shrugged, lowering his offered arm.

"Guess I'll catch you some other time," he said. "I hope we meet again, Carrie Carpenter of *The Daily New Yorker*."

"Thank you for tonight. I appreciated the company."

"Oh, believe me, the pleasure was all mine."

Carrie was shown to a much smaller and more intimate room. As she entered, the prince was standing, watching her approach, his eyes burning with that dark intensity that made her shiver. Breaking eye contact, he strode over to an antique mahogany cabinet, opening the doors and removing a decanter.

"Would you care for a brandy?"

"No thank you, I don't drink alcohol."

"Ah yes, the wine at dinner. I noticed you refused it. I wasn't sure if perhaps you just didn't care for it. You don't drink at all?"

"No, not at all," Carrie replied, wondering if refusing the wine had been such a big deal that she had been kept back to discuss it, like being held back by your teacher after class because you were in trouble.

"A soft drink then?"

"No, thank you, I'm fine. Prince …"

"Please, just call me Antonio; there is no need for such formality when we're alone."

He said the words, but he didn't drop his formal attitude. Carrie was nervous, not really sure what was going on, so she began to stroll around the room, examining the décor and artwork on display.

"I'm sorry; I should have explained why I wanted to see you, Miss Carpenter."

"Please, call me Carrie," she said, following his lead.

"I just wanted to thank you for all your help in this matter and let you know that I appreciate your actions."

Carrie whirled around to face him, not really sure what actions he was specifically referring to, but ready to brush them off with a not-at-all attitude. Her eyes went wide and her mouth formed a perfect o, her hand flying to her mouth to cover it as she heard a crashing sound to her right. Almost afraid to look, she turned and stared at the floor in horror. A burgundy and gold vase that had stood on a mahogany pedestal lay shattered on the marble floor, pieces scattered all around.

"Oh, my goodness," she almost cried. "I am *so sorry*; it must have been the dress. I'm not used to this full skirt...."

"Please, Miss...Carrie..." he almost seemed to savor her name as he spoke it for the first time. "Do not concern yourself so; it is only a trinket, not a precious family heirloom or priceless antique."

"I thought everything in the palace was an antique," she wailed.

"Well, perhaps, but it wasn't an important one. Please, come and sit with me for a moment."

Carrie was almost frightened to move in case her dress did any more damage, but she made her way to the brocade chaise lounge he had indicated, smoothing her dress down at the rear as she sat.

"Carrie, as you can imagine, I have been following almost every news report and article written on the matter of the Trayson Bay. I have to say I found yours to be most sympathetic and understanding of our plight. I was hoping for the chance to meet you at the conference to express our gratitude on behalf of the Spanish government. It seems also, after tonight, I must express personal gratitude to you for understanding that I was uncomfortable with the line of questioning, and for bringing the meeting back to the matter at hand."

"I wrote the articles only as I saw the situation, and my visit here has confirmed my assumptions and beliefs were correct; you have nothing to thank me for there. As for tonight, well, I am finding out that this business can sometimes be cutthroat, and people will take opportunities wherever they present themselves. I felt they were exploiting the situation too far, and feel I must apologize on behalf of my profession."

Antonio laughed, the sound rich and mellow, melting Carrie from the inside out. She felt a little giddy, as if she had drank all the wine offered at dinner. This didn't feel real—she was sitting in a room, alone with the heir to the throne of Spain! She had no idea how she had managed to form a sentence, never mind deliver that small speech.

"An ethical journalist, is that a first? I have to say I am even more impressed with you in person than I was with your articles. Carrie, would you do me the honor of joining my family for lunch tomorrow? By then, I will have met with the crews from Worldwide Disaster Cleanup and will know more about how they intend to handle the situation and the prognosis. I wish to give you, what's the term? The inside scoop."

"I'd be delighted."

The words were out of her mouth before Carrie even had a chance to think it over. How could she resist spending more time in his company, this man who made her feel things she had never felt before? She tried to tell herself that Mike would never forgive her if she passed up this opportunity, but the reality of the matter was she hadn't given the resulting article of insider information a single thought before accepting, concerned only with seeing him again.

"Wonderful. I will send a car to collect you at 2 p.m. Where are you staying?"

"The Westin Palace," Carrie replied dreamily as he rose and stood before her, resplendent in his formal attire.

"Perfect. Now I will arrange a car to get you back safely to your hotel; I believe you have an article to write, and I'm sure your editor will be anxious to receive it."

"Of course, yes!"

Carrie pulled herself from her daydreams of princes in fairy tale castles, taking the offered hand to rise. As her gloved hand met his, she felt that spark of electricity again, like a bolt from the blue. Her head swam and her breath caught in her throat. She swayed a little, and Antonio put an arm around her shoulders to steady her.

"Are you alright?"

"Yes, yes, I'm fine, thank you," Carrie said, a confused expression on her face. "I must have stood too quickly, that's all."

"Let's wait outside for the car; the fresh air will be good for you."

Walking to the door, Antonio offered her his arm to escort her as Pete had done earlier. She knew it would be rude to refuse, so she accepted, torn between loving the contact with this man and desperately needing to flee from it.

Once safely back in her hotel room, Carrie had a long soak in the tub, said her prayers, then curled up into bed, totally exhausted after the emotional day. Sleep just wouldn't come. Her mind kept straying back to the events she had experienced and the words of the prince. Antonio had called her an ethical journalist and had been surprised by the thought.

She had to admit, she herself had questioned this line of work, considering the strong moral code by which she was reared and which she had chosen as a guideline for her life. You heard such awful stories about some journalists at times, and there was doubt in her mind that she was truly cut out to join them. Having said that, her family name had provided an opening. She had also been given a natural talent for seeking possible solutions to problems and writing for understanding of those problems. She really believed there was a lot of good that she could do through writing.

More than that, though, Carrie had been strongly drawn to it, despite her reservations. That could only mean one thing for her; that it was the path she was meant to be on, no matter what the outcome. She might fail miserably through her inability to be ruthless and unscrupulous, but the failure would be in the terms of the judgment of man. People had decided that success was measured by power, affluence, and status symbols, and while a certain level of financial security was required in this life—after all, people had to pay their bills—it wasn't how Carrie saw things.

She felt that success should be determined by the amount of love, happiness, and contentment one could find within oneself. For her, those came from following God's will, and she knew He had a plan for her. Long ago, she had learned to open her heart to allow Him to guide her through this life, dealing with the things He chose to give her. Sometimes she could ponder over those reasons, perhaps even question them in her darkest moments, but she would never disobey or stray from where He led her.

She knew that everything in her life, be it heartache or happiness, held a lesson within that He wanted her to learn and understand. With each lesson she learned, she was one step closer to Him and His divine plan for her, and her eternal soul was more prepared for acceptance to his loving realm. On this plane of life, it wasn't for her to know that plan; she could only walk by faith and trust, knowing it would be revealed when the time was right.

Contemplating her walk through life with God, Carrie's thoughts went back to a song by Janice Kapp Perry that she learned in her young women's group. The final words always inspired her to be patient and follow His ways.

... And some day when God has proven me I'll see Him face to face. But just for here and now I walk by faith. Yes, just for here and now I walk by faith.

And that applied to this situation, too. She had no idea why God had put her in the path of this man, but she had faith that He had. Her mind was drawn to Antonio, and she was a little ashamed to admit that her body also seemed to be reacting to him in ways that were not appropriate, but it was more than that. Her very heart seemed to sing while in his presence, and she had the strong sense that he was the reason she was here now.

Carrie had done what she could in the plight of the wildlife; her country had listened and responded, and she could leave here very cheerful with that outcome. Now she was being asked to stay, and she wanted to. Was there more she could do professionally in terms of the disaster, or did she just want to spend more time with this man?

It seemed impossible that the two of them were intended to be linked in this life; they were incompatible in so many ways. They were miles apart, both geographically and in status. While she may be considered high society back in her home town of Midvale, perhaps even everywhere in the state of Utah, here and in New York, she was just a working girl, living on a monthly salary and trying to make ends meet like millions of others.

Not only was the prince heading for a brilliant political career, but he was royalty for goodness sake! He would be expected to marry within that realm, forming an alliance with another country, uniting their power and wealth, and producing heirs or heiresses with a true bloodline.

Carrie desperately hoped that love, marriage, and children were in God's plan for her life, but she knew that it couldn't be with this man. She had to consider why he had entered her life, or she had entered his. It seemed as if he was drawn to her too, but a casual dalliance was all he could offer, and that was something Carrie had no intention of allowing.

Then, of course, there was the most important matter of all—religion. She hadn't checked, but she assumed the royal family would be devout Catholics. Not being married in her own church, with a husband of the same religion, was just not in her game plan. She wanted to spend her life and eternity with a man who shared her faith. *Impossible fairy tale relationships! I just can't win.*

Carrie gave herself a shake, catching herself thinking of marriage with a man she had only met today. She knew Susan would say she was being utterly silly, and she was indeed. Surely it was all just a remnant of childhood fantasies, being rescued from a tower by her handsome prince. Perhaps that was the lesson that needed to be learned. That it was time to face up to those fantasies and let them go, allowing someone special, but ordinary in the eyes of the world, to steal her heart. *Susan will be happy to know I'm keeping my promise to 'think about it'. How can I not after the events of today!'*

Knowing that sleep was going to be impossible until she had talked this over with the two most important people in her life, she slid out of bed and reached for her phone, hitting the auto-dial for her mom's number.

"Hello, Sweetheart. I've been thinking about you. Are you having fun?"

"Oh, Mom, you won't believe what's happening to me. I was dressed in a beautiful gown for a dinner at the palace and personally met the prince."

"Tell me all about it."

Carrie continued to explain the day and the evening to her mom. Looking at the alarm clock, she realized more than twenty minutes had passed and she needed to have one more conversation before getting some sleep. So she concluded her conversation with the promise to finish telling her mom all about the trip when she got home.

"Good night, sweetheart. I love you and have confidence in your ability to make right choices."

"Yes, Mom, I know. . . .Remember who I am and what I stand for," she added, mimicking her mom. They both laughed at Carrie's recitation of the phrase her mom always told her children when they were leaving the house. "I love you, Mom. Good night." Carrie laughed at the memory of her mom always making sure they had a quarter in case they needed to call home while they were out. *How thrilled I was to finally get a cell phone so I no longer needed to rely on a pay phone or the quarter from Mom!*

Carrie put the phone down and knelt beside her bed for the second essential conversation. She prayed, asking for assistance in opening her eyes further to truly understand what she was supposed to do here in Madrid and what lesson God was trying to teach her or what service she was to render.

CHAPTER FIVE

Carrie felt much better when she awoke the next morning. She knew that God had heard her prayer and answered her. She felt much stronger and in control of her own emotions, and much more determined to keep this a professional relationship, focusing on the matter at hand. Anything else that needed to be done would be revealed in time, and God had granted her the patience to place her trust in Him. *I'll walk by faith.*

She had no hesitation in dressing in one of her most sensible black business suits with low pumps and a crisp white blouse with a high collar. Last night she had written what she considered to be one of the best articles of her career so far. Mike had emailed back immediately, telling her she was 'getting great stuff' and not to worry about her flight home, the ticket was open, and that she should 'stick with it while the going was good.'

Before leaving her hotel room, Carrie said a prayer of thanks. Despite her new resolve, her tummy still fluttered at the thought of the lunch with the prince and his family. This time, she could put it down to nerves. She didn't feel like she could eat breakfast, so she decided instead to write an email to Edith, updating her on events as promised. As she wrote, she wondered what gift she could take along for the royal family—turning up empty-handed seemed rude. What do you give someone who has everything? She settled for flowers. They were a simple gift, showing appreciation without being over the top, and nearly everyone enjoyed flowers.

Finishing her email to Edith, she decided to leave the hotel on foot rather than call a cab or Miguel. Later she would regret not asking Edith's or Miguel's advice on the gift.

It was in the heart of Madrid, after all, and she knew she wouldn't have to walk far before she found what she was looking for. Entering the flower shop, the amazing scents assaulted her senses, and the displays seduced her. Looking around, she was drawn to the beautifully delicate white lilies, looking regal in their refinement. She also loved the bright red color and the heady scent of the roses. She asked the florist to make up a display combining the two and was delighted with the result. The florist skillfully wrapped the large bouquet, then adorned it with red and white ribbons to match the flowers. Pleased with her shopping trip, she strolled back to her hotel, reaching the lobby only twenty minutes before the car was due to pick her up.

Entering the palace, she realized she didn't feel as nervous as she had before. The building was beginning to feel familiar to her, putting her at ease despite the company she was about to keep. She was led through to the drawing room, where the family sat, awaiting her arrival. As she entered the room, she approached the queen and presented her with the flowers, giving a tiny curtsy as she approached.

"So kind," Queen Isabella murmured, not looking in her direction and making no attempt to accept the gift. A giggle startled Carrie, and she was flustered as a butler dashed forward to take the flowers from her, removing them from the room. Antonio rose to greet her. Turning her away from the queen, he gestured to two teenage girls sitting together on the chaise lounge—the lounge where the prince had sat next to Carrie the night before.

"Allow me to introduce you to my sisters, Princess Catalina and Princess Adelina. I would like you meet Miss Carrie Carpenter."

He gestured to the pair as he spoke, and the older of the two, Catalina, giggled again while the younger nodded in acknowledgement.

"Catalina, please control yourself," Antonio said sharply.

"It's nice to make your acquaintance," the younger teen said.

Carrie was saved from further conversation by the announcement that lunch was ready. The king rose and offered one arm to Isabella and one to Catalina; Antonio copied the action, Carrie to his right and the younger princess, Adelina, to his left. Entering the same dining room as the evening before, the family took their places behind their chairs.

Spotting the only other place setting laid out, Carrie pulled out her chair to sit. A cough from behind her caused her to turn, and her friendly under-butler from the night before shook his head in warning. Carrie flushed as Catalina practically choked trying to contain her laughter. She may have been the older sister, but the younger one certainly had more presence and maturity. Utterly flustered by this time, Carrie was debating whether to sit or run as the family took their places in order of hierarchy. The choice was made for her as the under-butler stepped forward to hold her chair for her. She reluctantly took her seat directly across the table from Antonio and Catalina and, luckily, next to Adelina. The king and queen sat side by side at the head of the table.

This time, the under-butler served her water without her having to ask, and he winked at her as he placed her special carafe beside her glass. The friendly gesture helped her relax. After the food was blessed, she wasn't sure what to do next. Her tummy was rumbling due to lack of breakfast, but she was afraid to be the first to eat or drink. *I sure wish Edith had talked with me about proper table etiquette! I don't want Catalina laughing at me again.*

"So, Carrie," Antonio said as he sensed her quandary, "let me update you on the events of this morning." *What a relief! We can talk about something I know a thing or two about.* Noting the queen and king had begun eating, Antonio picked up his fork and motioned to her to do the same.

The rest of the lunch passed with them discussing the salvage team and the investigation, with the king and queen silently looking on and Catalina looking bored and snooty. Adelina said little but watched Carrie with questioning eyes. Carrie felt she had handled the situation well enough once the meeting turned to business, where she had a firm footing and was confident in her abilities. When the family rose to take their leave, Carrie stood politely. Adelina hesitated at the door and then rushed back to Carrie, giving her a quick hug.

"I'm sorry my sister was so rude. Thank you for being so charming."

With that, she hurried to catch up with her parents and sister. Astounded, Carrie turned to Antonio. "What was that all about?"

"Oh, my delightful, unassuming Carrie, you are a breath of fresh air. First, while it was very generous and considerate of you to bring a gift, it is not done when attending the royal palace, and the flowers you brought were inappropriate. Mostly, in European countries, lilies are for funerals only, and red is the color of revolution. For a country who so very recently had its streets run with blood, it would be considered an offensive gift, especially for the king and queen of that country. Then you almost sat before we did, but you weren't to know. Truly, it's my fault; I should have given you some guidance in advance."

Antonio looked startled as Carrie burst into peals of laughter. "I'm sorry," she gasped, seeing his shocked face. "It's just that I seem to go whole hog and get things *really* wrong. I don't do anything half-way!"

Antonio couldn't help but see the funny side, and the two laughed together, her tinkling laugh blending with his rich and mellow one, echoing around the dining room.

"I don't think this room has heard so much laughter in a long time," he said, sobering. "Carrie, before I get ahead of myself, would you allow me please to apologize for the behavior of Princess Catalina today. Her childish laughter was inexcusable under the circumstances."

"Please don't worry. I was a teenager once myself."

"I am terribly embarrassed by Catalina's self-centered behavior and will talk with her privately about it. At least my embarrassment was tempered by the more mature actions of Adelina—she is two years younger and more entitled to a lapse in behavior. Catalina is immature and interested only in what power and money can do for her."

"And then there is Adelina," he continued. "Of the two, she is the more mature and caring individual. She's a girl after my own heart, caring deeply for her country and her people. She's a quick study and has remained true to herself throughout her privileged upbringing, never becoming spoiled or taking anything for granted. She is truly the princess of whom I am most proud. Should the situation ever arise that one of my sisters be called upon to follow me to the throne, I pray it will be Adelina for the sake of my country. Again, my sincere apologies, Carrie."

"Apology happily accepted. Thank you for sharing your private thoughts with me."

"That's not all, Carrie. I have one more thing I must tell you. A confession, I'm afraid."

"A confession?"

"Yes. Did you wonder why *The Daily New Yorker* chose you to be the journalist who would represent them at this press conference?"

"I was surprised that I was chosen over the more senior reporters. I'm sure the others would have loved the opportunity to meet you and learn more about your country and particularly your work on the oil spill."

He looked into her eyes and somberly added, "My confession is simply that I asked for you to come."

"You *asked* for *me* to come? You didn't even know me."

"I knew your work, Carrie. Of course I read every word you had written about Spain, the oil spill, and our struggle to defend ourselves when Britain lashed out at us. And my heart was touched by the defensive stand you took on our behalf without even knowing us or having an agenda of any kind. I just had to meet the woman who could construct such a defense, a woman blessed with talent and intelligence, and with a heart that flowed through to her writing. So I specifically asked that you be sent here. Do you mind terribly?"

Carrie was surprised to learn he had personally asked for her to come, and her heart fluttered even more with the realization he was interested in her even before she came to Spain. "I don't mind at all. In fact, I'm very grateful for the invitation."

He gently raised her hand to his lips and touched it with the lightest of kisses; looking directly into her eyes, he added with barely a whisper, "Thank you for your forgiveness and understanding."

Carrie nodded and smiled, feeling a bit uncomfortable by the kiss. She let her hand slip back to her side and took a step backward to free herself from the closeness. *Be still my heart!*

"Now that I've unburdened my soul," he laughed, raising his eyebrows to lighten the mood, "Carrie, would you consider staying in Madrid for a few more days and being my official reporter on the upcoming events? You could attend the meetings and sit in on the conference calls."

"I will need to check with my editor, but I'm sure he will be delighted with the idea."

"What about you, Carrie? Would *you* be delighted with the idea?"

Antonio stepped closer to her, his eyes burning into her soul, one hand reaching up to run a fingertip down her cheek. Carrie was trapped in the intensity of his gaze, feeling like a deer in headlights as her cheek burned under his feather-light touch.

"I would," she breathed, before reminding herself where she was, and with whom she was visiting, not to mention her earlier determination to keep this strictly business. She took a step back, breaking the contact and the spell. "It would be extremely good for my paper to have access to the events as they unfold."

"Of course," Antonio said, stepping back and resuming his normal impassive expression. "Let me get you a copy of the schedule for the upcoming meetings."

The next few days passed like a whirlwind for Carrie. There were morning meetings, lunch meetings, afternoon meetings, and in between them all, she frantically wrote up articles to send back to Mike, who was over the moon to be able to have so many breaking stories. When she didn't have time to write the articles, she dictated them into her Dictaphone and uploaded the voice files, trusting one of the copywriters to type it up and get it ready for publication in time for the next issue. She knew the newspaper must be doing well out of this, and she was grateful for the opportunity to prove her worth to the company.

She also found the whole process fascinating and exciting, sometimes heartbreaking when there were birds or fish that couldn't be saved. As far as they could tell at the moment, the casualties were less than originally anticipated. All along the coastline, volunteers were trapping oil-covered birds and lovingly cleaning their feathers, the sicker ones transported to veterinary clinics where volunteers nursed them back to health whenever possible. New people flooded in every day—people from all walks of life and many different countries, offering their time and hard work.

To date the Galapagos Islands had been spared, and in addition to the satisfaction the volunteers got from being able to help, they received excessive accolades from Carrie in her articles. She quickly won the hearts of readers far wider than the newspaper distribution area. Every day after the paper had gone to print, her articles took pride of place on the website, and her following was becoming massive.

They worked together tirelessly. In addition to the work, Antonio always seemed to manage to fit in some time to spend alone with Carrie. Sometimes it would be lunch in between meetings at some quiet, out-of-the-way café or restaurant, where he would talk over the events and show great interest in how she was going to present her next article.

It always amazed her how the staff and owners would treat him with such respect and a slight hint of reverence, but they would still greet him warmly. They called him Don Antonio, the more casual form of address, and never showed any surprise or discomfort at having a member of the royal family occupying a spot in their establishments. They delighted to see him sharing tapas with an unknown American. She had finally plucked up enough courage to ask him about it one day.

He had looked surprised at the question, but he hadn't hesitated to answer. "As much as I'm a politician and a prince, I am also a man—a man who loves the city he lives in and likes to experience it. Although during official ceremonies there is a great deal of tradition that must be adhered to, and even as an ordinary man as I am today, I have to keep a certain level of decorum to my actions to avoid scandal. I always want to be a man of the people. I would hope there is not a single person in Madrid who would not greet me or approach me as they would any other familiar face. I do not put myself on a pedestal, thinking myself above them, and I do not fear for my safety among them. If they are unhappy with a decision, I would hope they would come and tell me about it, and where better than relaxing over good food! And with great company, I might add." His smile warmed her to her toes.

Carrie laughed along with him, but she was actually very impressed with his answer. It gave her a lot of food for thought, and she wondered if the prince would agree to an in-depth interview about him and his life as the heir apparent and what that meant to him. She took a deep breath and asked.

"There is not much to tell, Carrie," he shrugged. "My childhood was spent in a combination of being a normal, rowdy boy, and being trained in the proper etiquette required for public appearances and functions. When I was old enough, politics and economics were added to my lessons, as well as learning about military defense and strategy. I suppose I was groomed for this role, but in between, I did everything a normal boy would do. I played with my friends, sometimes fought in the schoolyard, climbed trees, rode bikes, fell off skateboards and came home with bloody knees. There is nothing there for your readers; I am not that interesting."

"But what does it really mean for you, being king?"

"I am not king yet, Carrie, and am not presumptuous enough to think ahead that way. My father has said privately that he will retire within the year and I will be crowned, but he may yet change his mind. The simple answer is that for me, the crown means only one thing: the opportunity to do good things for the people and to take care of the country they live in."

Wow, Carrie thought. *Either he's a genuinely wonderful man, or he is playing the role of diplomat well.* She didn't think it was the latter; he was relaxed, speaking in easy terms, the answers flowing, and Carrie could hear the sincerity within them. She knew her readers would actually go nuts for this stuff, but she hadn't actually received permission for the article. He was talking to her in private.

No matter how hectic the day had been, Carrie and Antonio always had dinner together, sometimes out in Madrid enjoying the buzzing nightlife around them and sometimes at the palace, but it was always informal, and they were always alone.

Carrie suspected that the king and queen didn't care for her much and wanted to avoid her, but that was okay with her. The formality required in their company was a bit much for her to take anyway. The more time she spent with Antonio, the more they got to know each other, talking about their everyday lives, exploring each other's pasts, learning about what lay beneath the exterior.

The more Carrie learned, the more she found to like, and she had to admit in excited calls to her friends back in New York, and in long emails to Edith, that she knew she was falling for him, and falling hard. Still she trusted God and walked the path, accepting that the loss of Antonio from her life would be something she would need to deal with when the time came. She knew that it would have to be soon; her real life was waiting for her back in New York, and she had no doubt that she would be called back to it shortly.

On the fourth night, just as she was about to leave Antonio and return to her hotel, he drew her into his arms. Powerless to resist, Carrie allowed herself to be held.

"Carrie," he breathed, as he stared into her eyes and stroked her porcelain cheek ever so lightly with his finger. "Can we keep denying this attraction we feel for one another? From the first moment I saw you in the conference room, lightness among a sea of darkness, shining like an angel, I have desired you. When you arrived for the dinner, you sent my senses reeling. You looked more like a princess than my own sisters. I had to look away, lest my admiration show too much and be noticed by others.

Then you intrigued me with your actions during dinner and your strange behavior with the wine and coffee, and you impressed me with your intelligence during the conversations. Then you go and act as my personal savior from the hyenas who wanted to pick apart the bones of my personal life. You are so beautiful, Carrie, and over these last few days I have learned that you are beautiful both inside and out. You have a radiance that shines from you, wherever you are, whatever you do."

Intoxicated by his words, Carrie was frozen in place as his head bent toward her and their lips met. The kiss was gentle, tender, and so very sweet. She felt her heart leap with joy and she sank into the sensations, causing him to gather her more firmly in his arms and deepen the intensity of the kiss. Carrie felt desire flare within her, an unfamiliar heat that started in her cheeks then burned its way down her body, inflaming her from head to toe and everywhere in between. Overcome with passion, she allowed the kiss to continue before she finally came to her senses and reluctantly but gently broke the connection.

Antonio continued to hold her and kiss her wherever he could, little butterfly kisses on her face, her neck, and her throat.

"Stay with me tonight, Carrie," he breathed in her ear, his voice a low and seductive murmur.

The words made Carrie shiver with pleasure, but they also brought her fully to her senses and she raised her hands to push him gently away. He looked at her quizzically, loosening the grip but not letting her go completely. He might be a great man, but he was a man, and he wasn't used to having his advances rejected. His strong good looks and lofty position normally assured him of success in that department.

"What's wrong, Querida? I was sure you felt the same way as I do. Our acquaintance has been brief, but the connection has been growing from the moment we laid eyes on each other, do you not agree?"

"I do, Antonio, but that kind of relationship isn't for me."

"What kind of relationship is that?"

"One that is fleeting, one where physical relations take place before marriage, one that has no hope of a future."

Antonio looked pained at her words. "Come back to the drawing room. Let's sit and discuss this properly."

Carrie followed, not even sure if she wanted to have the conversation, thinking perhaps it would be best if she just left. Considering how close they had become, he probably deserved a fuller explanation.

Sitting again on the chaise lounge together, the one they seemed to end up sharing frequently, Carrie explained to him all the reasons she had thought of a few nights ago as to why they could never be together. Antonio listened intently, his face patient, understanding growing as she spoke all her worries aloud for the first time.

"Then, of course, there is religion. You're Catholic and I'm a Mormon."

"Ah, now I understand the whole story behind the coffee and the alcohol. I thought you were perhaps, what do you Americans call it? A health nut!"

"Well, not quite," Carrie laughed. "But my body is a gift, and my doctrine advises on how to take care of it."

"Tell me more about this religion, the most important facts and the main beliefs."

Carrie did, and their discussion ranged from deep theological issues to lighthearted anecdotes. Antonio listened with great interest, asking her to share more.

"There are so many false claims about our religion. If you want to know more, ask someone who belongs to the church who actually knows and didn't hear it from a gossip mill. I will answer any question you have, and if I don't know the answer, I'll find it for you."

"For example, last year I was at an award ceremony for journalists. It was a lunchtime event in the height of summer, so I was wearing a bright orange sundress with a brightly flowered jacket. I was sipping my sparkling orange drink and having a great time. Our table of around twenty people was having a great time too, laughing and sharing stories. One person mentioned that someone in the industry was dating a Mormon. Of course, the conversation turned to the religion, and all the stories these journalists had heard, but not investigated, became the topic of discussion.

"I sat and allowed the discussion to go on for a while as the most ridiculous supposed Mormon beliefs were expounded as truth, things like Mormons only wearing black clothing, or not allowed to use modern appliances, or can't drive cars because they're taboo and so forth.

Finally after I felt I had given them 'enough rope to hang themselves,' as the saying goes, I cleared my throat and in as loud a voice as I could manage and still seem conversational, I declared that I was a Mormon, and here I was in my brightly-colored dress which I had steam-ironed that morning with an electrical appliance, was having lunch that was cooked with modern-day appliances, and, oh, by the way, if anyone needed a ride home afterwards, I had space available in my car and would be eager to give them a ride. You should have seen their faces!"

They talked and laughed easily together, but as their shared laughter brought them closer together on the intimate seat, the nearness was almost more than she could take. Her tummy fluttered; his smooth voice gave her goose bumps. *Is this really happening? No, it cannot be.*

The contact as he gently took her hands in his was accompanied by the stutter in her heart and the constricting of her chest, making it hard for her to breathe. Her palms felt warm and clammy, and she was embarrassed to think he would feel their condition and realize the effect the nearness was having on her. Carrie somehow managed to pull herself together and jumped to her feet. "I should go," she said nervously.

Antonio nodded, appreciating the great strength this lovely woman exemplified, and escorted her to the door, where the car was still waiting from her last attempt to leave. As they reached the car, he turned her gently by her shoulders to face him.

"Thank you, Carrie, for being so open and honest with me tonight."

He raised her hand to his lips and gently kissed her fingers before stepping past her to open the car door. As she lowered herself in, she caught the sadness in his eyes and he closed the door and turned away.

She too had a heavy heart as the car pulled out of the square and headed for her hotel.

CHAPTER SIX

The next morning as Carrie examined the upcoming schedule, she realized it would be time to go home sooner than she had thought. The plan to eliminate the oil spill and save the animals off the Ecuadorean coast was being implemented, meetings were beginning to die down, and oversight was the main job left to do. Everyone was more than confident that the spill was sufficiently contained to prevent its shift to the Galapagos and other important islands.

Carrie could find no reasonable excuse to stay much longer. It saddened her greatly, but it was also a relief in some ways. For the first time, real temptation had been placed in her path, and it had been an inner battle not to give in. She had admitted in her prayers that she thought she was in love with Antonio, and that she also desired him physically, as is natural in a loving relationship.

She knew that God would give her the strength to overcome, but it was also a kind of sweet torture to be that close, or be in his arms and know that the relationship could go no further and in fact would be coming to an abrupt end very soon.

During her last day in Madrid, Carrie finally took time away from Antonio and her work to visit the

Mormon temple up on the hill. The architecture of the building was primarily square lines and sharp edges, but it was beautiful in its construction—lines softened by the large, arched stained glass windows and decorative stonework and grounds. The towering spire adorned with the golden figure on top filled her with a sense of peace and joy, even as she approached.

Stepping inside felt like coming home, and she was filled with a sense of connection and contentment that filled her eyes with joyful tears. It had been too long since she had attended a temple service. Delightful memories of weddings and other occasions she had attended at various Mormon temples filled her mind, particularly the recent wedding of her cousin in the Mt. Timpanogos Temple not far from her family home.

She concealed a giggle as she remembered her cousin dropping his bride as he picked her up for a photo shoot outside the temple following their sealing ceremony. Putting memories aside, Carrie turned her thoughts to the service she was about to attend and her desire to know God's will in her life, especially concerning Antonio.

Later that day, parting with Antonio to head for the airport also filled her eyes with tears, but for very different reasons. They had spoken no more about the discussion they had on religion or a future together, and Antonio had respected her wishes, not pressuring her into more than she could give and keeping his kisses light and tender, almost chaste. There had been many of them though, and each had been bittersweet, with a sense of desperate finality. Silent tears had run down Carrie's cheeks for most of the seven-hour flight, and on more than one occasion, she'd had to squeeze into the tiny bathroom to sob. *Why am I putting myself through this? He'll soon be a king, a Catholic king! It can never work!*

She wasn't expected at the office after her long flight and was relieved to be heading home to the solitude of her tiny apartment. Her heart lifted when she arrived there to find two messages on her answering machine and three emails from Antonio. She stayed up until the early hours of the morning talking to him on the phone, both admitting to missing each other already.

Love had never been mentioned between them, but Carrie knew it was what she felt for him. She thought he might feel the same way, but she still couldn't see how they could have a future. His constant communications made it impossible for her to push him from her mind and life, so they continued on with their long distance relationship, with Carrie missing him more as each day passed.

She had talked with Susan while she unpacked and settled in, and after a short conversation they agreed to get together another time to allow Carrie the chance to talk with Antonio before going to bed. Her girlfriends, including Susan, were anxious for a night out to hear every detail about Carrie's trip in person, but with work commitments and their hectic schedules, it was almost two months before they all found space available in their planners to get together. Susan, Janet, Angela, and Carrie finally met late on a Saturday afternoon at their favorite wine bar, where her friend Susan made her usual joke ordering drinks from the bartender.

"Three glasses of the house red please, and one white wine spritzer, but hold the wine."

The bartender was familiar with the girls and laughed, pleased to see the group together again in his bar. He happily prepared their drinks, adding a strawberry to the bottom of the champagne flute he filled with clear soda for Carrie. He presented it to her with a flourish, as if to say, 'Don't get too loaded on this one, Honey!' She giggled as she thanked him, looking forward to an easy night of laughter and fun, a chance to unwind and just enjoy the company of her friends.

Taking their usual spot, the three friends proceeded to ask a barrage of questions; Carrie held up her hand for them to stop.

"Whoa, Team! I can only answer one question at a time," she gasped through her laughter at their eagerness.

"Okay," Susan grinned. "Why not just tell us the whole story from start to finish. And don't leave anything out, especially the juicy details!"

"Fair enough," Carrie said, and told them absolutely everything about the trip, having them dabbing at tears one minute, and helpless with laughter the next. As she finished with the blow-by-blow bringing them up to date with her life, the girls sat in silence looking thoughtful.

"By the sounds of this, things with this guy could be the real deal, right?" Janet asked her.

"I don't know." Carrie shook her head, not sure how to explain her feelings. "I know I miss him, want to be with him, and think about him all the time, and when we're together, it feels magical."

"The girl is definitely in lurrrvvee," Susan joked.

"What I don't get," Janet, ever the pragmatist, interjected, "is why you don't just overcome the obstacles? It doesn't sound that hard to me." *Here she goes again, always the devil's advocate.*

She waved her glass of red wine in the air, about to embark on one of her famous speeches. "First of all, you're not exactly a bum, Carrie. You are actually very high society when you look at your family back home. You don't really need to work, so you could just move to Madrid and play the role of wife. After all, that English prince married what they call a commoner. She's of 'excellent breeding' as the papers say, but she has no connection to royal blood. The family has accepted her, and the British people seem delighted with her; who's to say it couldn't be the same for you?"

"If that were the only problem, you might just be right and it would be worth considering, but it's more complicated than that," Carrie mock groaned, loving her friends' way of viewing the world but knowing problems couldn't be solved that easily. "I have no idea what the real story is behind this Swiss princess—no amount of digging has turned up if they are actually promised to each other or are just good friends, and I haven't dared ask him. Considering I got so annoyed with the other journalists for probing about that very thing, it wouldn't have been right to do the same! Besides, I can say he likes me and is attracted to me, but I've no idea how deep that runs with him. He's a prince; he probably has silly little girls throwing themselves at him all the time!"

"Yeah, but you're not a silly little girl," Angela interjected. "You are a strong, independent, financially secure woman who knows her own mind, not some bimbo blinded by the fact that he's a prince."

"I wouldn't be so sure; you should have seen him in his official dress and regalia!"

They all laughed along with Carrie, but Susan, probably the closest to Carrie and the one who knew her the best, soon looked at Carrie with sympathy and understanding. "It's also the religious aspect, isn't it?"

"Yes, that's kind of a major stumbling block. He's Catholic, which means we could never get married. It's not that he's Catholic per se, but without being baptized into my church, he can't even go inside the temple with me, and the Spanish king must be Catholic," she answered sadly.

"Why don't you just convert?" Janet asked. "Surely all Christian religions are based around similar teaching and tenets; it shouldn't be that hard."

Carrie sighed, trying to think of a way to explain her inner feelings to her friends. "Well, in a way perhaps they are, but I was born into and raised in my beliefs, and attending the temple is an important part of my faith. No other religion would feel right for me, and turning my back on being a Mormon would be like betraying the God who has loved me and cared for me all my life. It can't be done, not by me. Even if I could, I would never truly embrace another religion, and that would be like mocking God by going through the motions, pretending to be something I'm not. I have always been, and will always be, a Mormon."

"If you say so," Janet said easily. "Why not just forget about marriage and still share a life together? You can still live together, have a family, worship together, just not in each other's churches."

The three girls laughed at Janet's pragmatic viewpoint, but Susan rushed to her friend's defense. "I don't think living in sin would be an option for a Mormon or a Catholic, or for the royal family, Janet."

"Yeah, yeah, so what then? Seems to me like he would have a lot more to lose if he was going to be the one to convert—his religion, his throne, his political career, and his family. Isn't that a bit selfish and unfair to expect him to do that?"

"It would be," Carrie agreed. "Totally unfair and selfish, and I don't expect him to do any of that, nor would I ever ask it of him."

Janet put a hand on Carrie's arm. "I know you might think I'm giving you a tough time, but I care about you a lot, and I don't want to see you get hurt. You've fallen for him in a big way and your heart wants him, but you know that it can never be. I just want you to realize how impossible it is before you're in too deep. You should put him out of your mind, put an end to the communication and move on, for your own sake."

Easy for her to say. She doesn't love him.

"I know," Carrie nodded. "Believe me, it's been my intention for a long time, but I just can't do it. We talk every day, several times a day. We text. We email. All till late into the night. It's a wonder either of us has time to work."

"Enough," Susan said. "I think you've grilled Carrie about all she can take for one night, Janet. This is supposed to be a fun night out remember? Carrie, tell me again how you messed up at the lunch with the whole family, that's just so funny!"

The cheerful mood reestablished, the girls proceeded to enjoy their night out, the ambience of the wine bar and good company relaxing them from the stresses of the hectic pace of city life. Although the other girls checked out the smartly suited clientele, Carrie refrained from joining in, knowing there was no other man in the whole of New York City, or perhaps the world, to compare to Antonio Francisco Javier Carlos Dominguez.

After having their fill of the sophisticated setting, the girls weren't nearly ready to call it a night. Deciding that dinner was definitely in the cards, they debated loudly over where they would go, considering no one had made any reservations. Carrie decided to go with the flow and left the others to it since they knew the city better than she did. She was learning, but there was a lot to come to grips with, and things changed at such a constant pace she sometimes couldn't keep up. What had been a nice, distinctive Italian restaurant last week could very well be a health juice bar the next time they decided to go out. It was all just part of living in this exciting city, and she had learned to embrace it.

She followed her friends outside, not sure where they were heading since her mind had been on Antonio and their relationship. Flagging down a cab hadn't reached the level of impossibility that would occur later that night, so it was a good time to be moving on.

Arriving at the restaurant, Carrie was pleased with the choice. Opening the door, they were greeted by the wonderful smells of cooking, and she was surprised to realize she was ravenous. She giggled to herself as she remembered the last time she was this hungry, not knowing when it was appropriate to begin eating at the royal family's table. *Sugar cubes! Why does everything bring me back to thinking of him?*

Chiding herself for bringing him foremost into her thoughts yet again, she pulled herself firmly back to the present and her friends. They were seated at a table for four at the side of the room. She eagerly accepted the menu from their server with thanks, then dove into the conversation about what each was going to choose and what they could share. Food ordered, the girls proceeded to fill Carrie in on what she had missed from their lives over the past few weeks.

She was startled when halfway through her meal, a shadow fell across the table.

"Hi, Carrie, I thought that was you. It's Pete, from Madrid."

"Of course, Pete Barker, *Economist Weekly*," she grinned. "Nice to see you again. What brings you to New York?"

"I'm following up on a whisper about some possible insider trading going on in the stock market. I've got quite a few meetings set up so I'm in New York for a week at least. I'm hoping to have some free time, and to be honest, I was thinking that I'd love to catch up with you while I'm here."

"Great," Carrie replied. "I'm sure we'll manage to squeeze in something."

She had liked the man and enjoyed his company that night at the palace. Finding a free lunch hour to show him some sights or a night to do dinner should both be fun and provide opportunity for them to continue to discuss developments and progress with the oil spill. She looked forward to learning more about the economic fallout from it.

"That's good; I've been thinking about you a lot, Carrie."

Suddenly her friends were silent, with all eyes fixed firmly on Carrie, who was taken by surprise. She might be innocent and sometimes a little naïve, but she couldn't fail to miss the change in tone and the intensity in Pete's expression. Now spending time with him didn't seem such a good idea and she blushed, not really sure how to address his comment.

To be honest, other than responding politely to the email she had received from him thanking her for a delightful dinner and congratulating her on the breaking stories she had written, she hadn't given the man a single thought. She felt three pairs of curious eyes stare at her from around the table, so she used a distraction technique to avoid addressing the connotations of his remark.

"Oh, where are my manners? Ladies, this is Pete Barker, a journalist from Washington. We met while we were both in Madrid. Pete, this is Susan, Janet, and Angela." She motioned to each in turn, giving them 'the look.'

They all made nice-to-meet-you noises, and overcome with politeness, Carrie reluctantly asked if he would care to join them.

"Oh, no, I couldn't possibly. In fact I'm sorry to intrude on your dinner, but I was just leaving and couldn't go without stopping by. It was nice to meet all of you, but I'd better take my leave. Carrie, I'll email you and we'll see what we can set up," he delivered as his parting shot, retreating from the table.

"Yes, of course," she replied weakly as he departed. She didn't relish the thought that the friendly acquaintance had seemed to shift gears, but knew it would be rude to change her mind so suddenly after just agreeing to spend time with him.

Susan laid down her fork decidedly. "Carrie, have you been holding out on us? Have you just gotten yourself into another crazy situation or is this a fairy tale-come-true kinda guy, too? Come on, time for the gossip!"

Carrie made it home just minutes before midnight, which was late for her. After dinner, which had been early by New York standards, the girls had wanted to go dancing and Carrie had decided that what the heck, she was only young once. It was the weekend, and she had nowhere else to be or any responsibilities to fulfil that night.

They had danced and laughed, sticking close together, careful not to give off any signals to say they were available to any of the single men or weirdoes that hoped to hook up in these places. Of course, some had tried, but the feisty Janet and the quick-witted Susan had soon sent them packing, leaving them in no doubt that their advances weren't welcome.

She'd had a lot of fun, but now Carrie was exhausted and her feet were aching; all she wanted to do was change clothes, say her prayers, and crawl into bed. She glanced longingly at her laptop, wondering if there were emails waiting for her from Antonio, but she really needed to check on some preparations for church tomorrow. She had done most of it earlier but intended to finish it when she got home, not expecting it to be this late.

By the time she finished what she needed to do for church the next day, she was more than ready for bed. Completely forgetting she had turned her cell phone off in the wine bar, she placed her dark and silent device on the bedside table, knelt down to say her prayers, and crawled gratefully under the comforter where she fell asleep almost instantly, with no clue of the number of missed calls on her phone.

CHAPTER SEVEN

While Carrie was crawling into bed, Antonio was pacing around his dressing room. It was 7 a.m. on Sunday morning in Madrid, and despite the messages he had left on Carrie's phone and the texts and emails he had written, he had heard nothing back from her since Saturday morning New York time. It wasn't like her not to reply, and his mind was conjuring up all sorts of scenarios.

Maybe she had been in an accident and was hurt or in the hospital. Panic flared through him at the thought, the idea of her even having so much as a scratch abhorrent to him; he wanted to shield her from everything negative in this world, to protect her and care for her as if she were a delicate flower. These last three months had been the best of his life, and he'd become addicted to their almost constant contact through technology.

However, that was just one of the explanations his fevered mind was inventing. As it roamed elsewhere, he sizzled with fury at the idea she might have been out on a date with another man. She was his! He should be the only man that she spent time alone with, and the thought of that not being the case filled him with a jealousy so deep, it set fire to every nerve ending in his body.

There were only two possible explanations for her silence that were acceptable to him, and those were if she had been tied up with something important to do with her work or had a family emergency. He greatly admired the skill and compassion she displayed in her articles, and he read each one with a sense of pride. He had been watching the paper's website, but there was nothing new being posted that was written by Carrie. Unable to stand the confines of his bedroom suite any longer, he fled the palace, asking his butler to summon his driver as he left.

Once the car pulled up outside, Antonio dismissed the driver, took the keys, and left on his own. He knew his parents would be furious with him for doing so, but at this moment, he didn't care. It broke some sort of etiquette for the prince to move around the city unaccompanied, leaving him open to danger and possible allegations of scandal.

But Antonio often tired of the restrictions placed upon him every second of every day. He knew that the drivers doubled as security—and without Pedro by his side, anything could happen—but he was certain he was safe in his own city. Today, he just wanted to drive. He enjoyed driving and got to do it so rarely; it relaxed him and helped him think, and he most definitely needed to think right now.

His worry over Carrie was still present, but what he needed to consider deeply were his reasons for the passionate emotions aroused by his thoughts. Before he had ever laid eyes on her, he had known from her articles that she was intelligent, with a quick wit and sharp mind. He had also determined that she was fair and compassionate, and, between the lines, he could sense her loving nature. He had been impressed and grateful with how she had treated the reputation of the Spanish government in the coverage of the story, and he had meant to seek her out at the press conference to tell her so. He'd deliberately ensured *The Daily New Yorker,* and Carrie specifically, were invited for that very reason.

When he had stepped up to the podium and looked over the audience, Antonio had somehow known straight away that the blonde woman dressed demurely in a cream-colored outfit was Carrie Carpenter. He couldn't explain how he knew, but he did. It was as if he could match the words he had read with the woman he saw before him. There seemed to be a radiance about her, something shining from within that couldn't be contained. In his mind, Antonio associated it with the sincerity and compassion she displayed in her writing. Her intelligence shone from her eyes, and the casual grace of her small movements hinted at breeding and education, as did her articles. He was in no doubt that this was the woman he sought.

The only thing that had taken him completely by surprise was her beauty. Sometimes the women who were beautiful on the outside were perhaps not so beautiful on the inside. He had not expected her to be angelic in her loveliness, naturally exquisite, requiring little artificial adornment. The reasons behind the dinner invitation had been genuine, but he was overjoyed that she could legitimately be included in the invitation.

She had surprised him again that night, having taken time and effort to discover and adhere to the requirements of the unexpected engagement. The staff had been informed to check over the guests and assist those who required it. Carrie had needed no such help and had looked stunning in the formal wear, like a fairy tale princess come to life. He'd found it very hard to concentrate on his obligations that night, his attention being drawn on multiple occasions to her end of the table.

Antonio had to admit he had been completely enchanted with her from the moment she had been so distressed over that silly vase. He didn't dare tell her that it probably was some priceless antique, a gift from another nation; she might have fainted on him! From that moment on, everything he had done had been built around spending time with her while still keeping his commitments.

He hadn't questioned his motives, and even if he had, he knew he would have made excuses to himself as well as others. It was time to face up to them. There was no doubt he liked her a lot and wanted her physically. When she had made it clear that wasn't going to happen, why did he persist with seeing her as much as he could? Why had he continued to keep in contact with her several times a day once her assignment was over and she had returned to her own country?

He thought it all through as he was driving, recalling every word she had said, every question she had asked, every movement, every nuance, the delightful scent of her hair, how her eyes sparkled when she laughed. Antonio pulled over and stopped the car, overwhelmed with the memories. Putting his head in his hands, he groaned. There was only one explanation: in the short time they had been together; he had fallen head over heels in love!

He stayed that way for several moments, contemplating the situation. He knew exactly how much being king meant to him. It meant the chance to help his people, fighting for them and acting as an ambassador for their country, improving their relationship with the rest of the world. The rest of it didn't matter to him that much.

He didn't care for the pomp and ceremony, he didn't care about the status or the riches, and he certainly didn't care for the fawning of those that sought him out only because of his title. Could he possibly forsake his chance to care for his people to care for just one person instead? He pondered over the possibility.

If he renounced his claim to the throne, then Catalina would be next in line. As much as he loved his sister, he had to admit her shortcomings. She had displayed some of them when she first met Carrie at the Palace. Catalina was shallow and self-centered, having allowed the power and position she held to affect her, considering it her right. It showed immaturity and internal weakness, and she would not make a good queen. He would worry for his people if it came down to her ruling.

He laughed at the devilish thoughts that were entering his mind. *Yes, Catalina would not make a good queen today, but what if she married someone who could help her grow up, be more responsible and far less selfish and immature? No, she's not going to change. Title and wealth are all that concerns Catalina. No, I simply could not do that to the country I love.*

Antonio's mind was in a whirl—there was so much to consider. It was such a complex situation, and he hadn't even begun to contemplate all of it yet. Would his family completely disown him if he asked to take a bride, a future queen, whose heritage was not the proper bloodline just because he loved her? And would his people shun him for such an action? These were important considerations for him.

Then there was the matter of religion. He had been reading all that he could on the subject of Carrie's religion and everything he read rang true to him. She had explained some of the basic teachings to him one night, but other than his reading and her explanation, he didn't yet have a deep understanding of her beliefs and doctrines. *But if her religion means so much to her, and if I love her, then her religion must mean as much to me. Am I to lose this woman I love because of our religious differences? God help me!*

All his life he had learned of no religion except Catholicism. He had been raised in the Catholic faith, and it was intrinsically linked to Spain and to his family, going back as many generations as he could find documented. Was that something else he could find the strength to walk away from? If he joined Carrie's religion, could he fully embrace it, or would he be doing himself, Carrie, and God an injustice by converting just to be with her, while inside remaining true to Catholicism?

Whoa! Aren't you getting ahead of yourself? Of course, he was. He had no idea if Carrie returned his feelings or would even want him. *Where do I turn from here?*

It was Sunday, and although he knew his priest would be busy, Antonio decided he needed to see him now. Starting his car, he headed toward the church he had attended most of his life. Although the principle diocese was the Catedral de Santa María la Real de la Almudena, which was located right next to the royal palace, he didn't consider it his church, despite attending it on many occasions. The building had been started in 1883, but it had never been completed and was only consecrated in 1993. As such, Antonio had grown up attending the Church of San Isidro el Real, and even on completion of the new building, Father Marcos had preferred to stay loyal to his church and congregation. As far as Antonio was concerned, his church was wherever Father Marcos was.

Pulling in where he could easily park, Antonio took a stroll on his way to the cathedral. It was too early to disturb his priest, but already the city was busy with older generations who liked to be out of bed and on the go first thing. They gathered at street cafés for a light breakfast with friends and family before fasting for Mass. Some drank tiny mugs of strong black coffee, often with a glass of water or a small brandy alongside. Others indulged in the traditional breakfast of hot chocolate and churros, small choux pastry concoctions that were deep-fried but unsweetened, making a delicious savory accompaniment to the sweet beverage. Many were engrossed in the conversations at their tables, but those that noticed Antonio hailed him heartily with warm greetings and smiles coming from every direction. He returned every one, berating himself for not finding the time to do this more often. It felt wonderful to be so free, and he wished he had the time to stroll, to sit down whenever he felt like it at the almost constant stream of cafés that lined the streets.

His current life didn't provide those luxuries, and to be honest, he couldn't think of a single person who would have the time to share the experience with him. Although he probably had thousands of acquaintances, his life was such that as an adult, he had very few close friends. The only one he could truly name in this capacity was Father Marcos.

Reaching the building, he pushed open the heavy doors. He knew they wouldn't be locked, especially on a Sunday. Entering, he dipped his fingers into the font of holy water and crossed himself. The intricacy and ornateness of the inner building awed him as always, the feeling of powerful serenity washing over him as he approached the sanctuary, where the highly decorated altar and tabernacle were situated. He genuflected before them and offered a prayer before returning to a pew and taking a seat. The church was empty since mass was not scheduled for another two hours.

"Well, well, Antonio my friend. What brings you here so early today?"

Antonio turned to face the welcome voice, smiling affectionately at the small man making his way toward him. In his ever-efficient way, he was already dressed in most of the outfit required to perform the ceremony later.

"I had hoped to see you, Father Marcos, unless you are too busy since it is Sunday."

"All my preparations are finished and everything is ready. Besides, I'm never too busy to see you. I am curious, though. Is there something wrong? Is the family well?"

"Yes, we are all fine; there are no concerns on that score. You won't be giving me the last rites anytime soon." He grinned at his friend.

"You shouldn't make light of such matters, Antonio."

Despite his words, the priest couldn't help but laugh at Antonio's words and cheeky grin. He had known him since birth, and Father Marcos often saw flashes of the small, impish boy he had been while under his tutelage.

"I know, but even you have to admit that the church takes itself a little too seriously sometimes."

"Well, I suppose I can admit that, but is that what you came here to discuss at the break of dawn on a Sunday morning? Was it so important for you to try to get me to see the funny side of my religion?"

The priest was smiling, but Antonio could see the concern in his eyes. Years of being in this position had taught him endless patience, and he would never push him to talk.

"There is a matter of great importance I need to discuss with you," he finally said quietly.

"Is this a conversation between friends, or one with your God with your priest in attendance?"

"Both. I need it to be both."

"Then come through the Chapel of Our Lady of Good Counsel and let her guide me in assisting you."

The chapel was a much smaller and more intimate room, with only a handful of wooden pews and a solid gold altar that stretched high up to the domed ceiling. A statue of La Macarena resided there, looking serenely down upon the pews, waiting to advise all who came to her.

Once settled there, Antonio told Father Marcos the entire story of his meeting with and subsequent feelings for Carrie. He poured out the turmoil of thoughts and concerns, explaining everything he was feeling as best as he could. Coming to the end, he sighed; when all told, the situation seemed hopeless.

Father Marcos looked a little stunned, but he sat back in his seat, contemplating his answer and waiting for guidance. He must have received it, as he soon spoke with confidence.

"Antonio, in the matter of the crown, you must speak with your father. He is not a stupid man, and if he is aware there is even a possibility of you renouncing your position, he will make the correct decision regarding Catalina. Whether she should make a match to rule Spain or marry for other reasons is a decision that does not need to be yours alone. You are burdening yourself unnecessarily if you do not confide in him. You have already shared this burden with God; now share it with another man who holds the same values and responsibilities as yourself."

"You're absolutely right," Antonio nodded. "I was feeling too guilty to even think of that. Of course, the decision should be made together."

"As for the rest, Antonio, as your friend, I am so happy you have finally fallen in love, and I hope dearly that this woman returns your affections. As your friend and your priest, you know I cannot advocate you turning your back on your religion, no matter how joyous the circumstances. If you have come for my blessing, I cannot give it."

Antonio's face fell. He realized that deep down he had hoped his friend would give his blessing, telling him that as long as he remained faithful to God and true to himself, the nature of the building in which he worshipped wasn't an issue, nor was the name of the religion.

"Having said that," the priest continued. "I suggest you look deep into your own heart. Think about the differences as well as the similarities between the two religions, pray, and speak to yourself honestly about what you believe to be the right path. Do not accept a religion just to be with this woman, for a false God is abhorred by all. Is there anything in particular—other than the girl—that speaks to your heart about this church?"

Antonio nodded. "I have to admit, my experience so far is limited, but from my research, what appeals to me greatly is the sense of family and community they have together. It's difficult to explain, but they truly seem to live by their doctrines, applying them to every aspect of their lives. It's a total immersion into their beliefs, and their whole way of being is shaped by their love and dedication to God and Jesus Christ, never giving in, no matter what the temptation. It's why I know Carrie would never convert, and I couldn't ask her to. Without her religion, she wouldn't be the same person; she wouldn't be the girl with whom I have fallen in love."

Father Marcos had watched Antonio closely during his little speech. He patted him on the shoulder as he stood. "Will you stay for Mass and take Holy Communion with me today, Antonio, while your heart is still true to the faith?"

Antonio was shocked by the words. He loved his church and his priest. He had only thought he was looking at the situation logically with his head for the moment, trying to discover if there was a way to make it work. He hadn't considered that his simple exploration into another religion might lead him to be untrue to his church.

"Of course, I will, Marcos."

He rose and the men hugged briefly.

"I suggest you remain here in solitude until it is time. Pray to God and to Our Lady, ask them for guidance and help in allowing the scales of confusion to fall from your eyes, revealing the truth within your heart clearly to you. Listen carefully to their answers, for I think they might surprise you. I will always be your friend, Antonio, even if someday I am no longer your priest."

With that, Father Marcos departed, leaving Antonio alone with his thoughts and torn emotions in the intimate beauty of the chapel. When he finally departed the church that day and walked to his car, he knew his decision would separate him in some way from one he loved—either Marcos or Carrie.

Janice Limb Myers

CHAPTER EIGHT

Carrie was having a dream wherein she sat on a bench in Central Park, bundled up in her thickest winter clothing, watching two dark-haired and dark-eyed children ice skate.

"Look what I can do, Mommy!" the little boy cried, waving. Carrie raised her arm and waved back before a shrill, piercing beep almost deafened her, causing her to cover her ears with her gloved hands and screw up her face.

Groggily Carrie awoke and found herself completely entwined in her snuggly comforter and linens. *So this is what it feels like to be a burrito.* The noise continued to assault her ears as she struggled to extract a hand from the tangle she had created while she slept. Finally locating her arm and fingers, she managed to reach the alarm and shut it off. She flopped back onto the pillows, exhausted with her efforts even before she had made it out of bed. Carrie had no idea what she had been doing through the night to get herself into this pickle. Maybe she had been ice skating too, flinging her arms and legs about in impressive twirls and jumps. She could feel the grin cross her face as she remembered the dream and the adorable kids that seemed to be hers. Her smile faded at the realization that there was no doubt who the father of them would be in dreamland, not with those looks, and in dreamland was where they would always stay. She sighed as she began to unravel herself from the bedclothes.

Showered, dressed and standing in the kitchen gulping a glass of orange juice, Carrie finally felt more awake and alive. She grinned to herself as she thought of how much worse her friends would feel, having added alcohol to the pounding music and the sleep deprivation. She wickedly considered giving each of them a call at this early hour just to pay them back for their constant teasing the night before. No, she wouldn't do that to them, not really, but it was a fun thought.

She glanced at her laptop but realized she didn't have time to boot it up right now. Sunday was a day she reserved for her worship, service, and family. Not her blood family—they were too far away, although she often wished she were close enough to drop in on them for a casual visit—but for now she had a church family and a position of responsibility in that family. Carrie was the Relief Society President in the Manhattan Young Single Adult Ward, which meant she was responsible for running the women's organization as a volunteer and also caring for those in need, particularly the women. Today after church, a few of the single girls were going to stay together and relax with a light lunch in the park. So she set to work cutting bread and cheese, carefully wrapping it and placing it neatly in a picnic basket. She added bottles of water and some pieces of fruit before closing the hamper, satisfied with her work. Laying her juice glass in the sink to deal with later, she grabbed her cell phone and scriptures and headed for her car.

Arriving at the Manhattan church, she saw Valerie waving to her frantically from the doorway of the building. Having to drive on to find a parking spot, she hurried back toward the building on foot, concern for her friend filling her thoughts.

"Carrie, thank goodness! I was trying to call you last night but your phone was going straight to voice mail."

"I'm sorry. I had it turned off while I was out with friends. What's wrong, Valerie?"

"Oh, there's nothing wrong with me, I just wanted to ask you a few questions about the cooking club we're putting together. I was worried about you because I couldn't get hold of you; you always have your cell phone on!"

Carrie laughed in relief but decided she'd better have a quick glance at her phone. Sure enough, it was still switched off from the night before. She turned it on and saw the icon on the screen telling her she had fourteen missed calls. Accessing the missed call log, she saw four from Valerie and Antonio's name filling the rest of the display. She smiled as she saw his name, not bothering to check the log further. She would speak to him later in the evening, but for now she needed to immerse herself in her worship. She turned the phone off again and walked inside with Valerie.

Three hours later, a group of beaming women left the church. Carrie had remained to consult with one of the women having a problem, and the others waited outside in the fresh air. Soon Carrie joined them to drive to the park to have lunch together and discuss the assignments for the cooking club. It was beginning Thursday night, and they would take turns each week teaching each other how to make their favorite recipes.

As single girls living in a vibrant city filled with places to eat out, learning to cook hadn't really been a priority for many of them, although they all knew a few staple recipes passed down by their mothers. They were all keen to share what they knew and to learn from the others. If marriage was in the cards for them, they wanted to be good wives and mothers, and cooking was a large part of that.

They needed to finalize some of the details, and they agreed that doing so during a walk in Central Park was perfect. The early October weather was comfortable for walking, and there was no better time or place to appreciate the beauty of nature God had provided them than Central Park in the fall. The rich and varied palette of colors created a stunning sight designed by God to fill one with wonder and joy.

They carpooled to the park, and Carrie spent the rest of the afternoon in the bosom of her second family, strolling along and talking while enjoying the view. They stopped to sit on a bed of fallen leaves, sharing scriptures as they nibbled on the simple fare Carrie had provided for them and then discussed the club, firming up the details they hadn't decided on yet.

It was early evening when a cheerful Carrie arrived home. She emptied out the picnic basket, discarding the trash and placed the dishes neatly away before checking through her phone messages. She remembered she had checked earlier and seen several listed from Antonio. Her heart fluttered. She truly missed talking with Antonio, even for two days.

Her mood dropped when the second screen of the call log showed several missed calls from Mike. She gulped, wondering what she might have missed. She and Mike had an understanding, an unwritten agreement that she would be on call twenty-four-seven to cover any breaking stories, except from midnight on Saturday to midnight on Sunday.

It had worked very well to date, and Carrie had been careful to tell him on Saturday morning at the office that she was cutting out at 4 p.m. that afternoon and having a night out with her friends. It had been the first time she'd taken time off since she'd started at the paper, and she felt she deserved it.

Mike hadn't even glanced up from his screen to acknowledge her comments but had merely muttered something that sounded a lot like "Yeah, yeah, sure thing," and waved her out of the office. She had taken that to mean he didn't care and was fine with it. Now she returned his call, anxious about why he was trying to get hold of her. Instead of answering the call like a normal human being, a voice bellowed in her ear when the call was picked up at the other end.

"Where the heck were you last night?"

Carrie's heart sank. Her boss obviously hadn't been listening to her, and she was in trouble for the first time.

"I was out, remember? Saturday morning I went into your office to tell you I was having a night out and would be turning my phone off."

She tried to sound diplomatic, explaining herself without being defensive.

"I never agreed to that!" Mike exploded. "I needed you to work and I couldn't get hold of you. Journalists can't just swan off whenever they feel like it, Carrie. News happens no matter which day of the week it is. If you don't realize that, then perhaps this isn't the career for you!"

"Now," he continued, "the Greenpeace bunch in Britain are blocking the highways and picketing the imports of all goods coming in from Spain. I need you on it, and I need your article by 4 a.m. so it can go to print in Monday's paper."

"Couldn't someone else have covered the story?"

"Yes, they could, but that's not the point. You're the one who has been the bleeding heart sympathizer all through this thing; our readers will want *your* opinion on this development, not anyone else's. Stop wasting time arguing and get it done! We're already behind the TV news and other papers on this one."

Carrie winced; Mike was really mad at her, even though this wasn't really her fault. There many good copywriters at *The Daily New Yorker,* and at the push of a button he could have gotten one of the others to emulate her tone and writing style. She wouldn't have minded if an article had gone out with her by-line as long as they stuck to her values and usual fair assessment of the situation. Mike obviously considered this an emergency, and exceptions should be made in emergencies.

"Mike," she almost whispered. "It's Sunday."

"I don't care what dang day it is!" Mike roared into the phone, forcing Carrie to hold it away from her ear. "I've been more than tolerant of this 'can't work on a Sunday' bull crap you pull with me, but this time, I don't care if the Pope himself is sitting having tea in your house right now. Forget the religious crap and get to work." He slammed down the phone.

Carrie listened to the phone go dead and sat down wearily at her kitchen table. Tears pricked her eyes, not from sadness, but from disappointment and anger. She had never been in trouble this way before, at any point in her life. Never had someone been so angry with her that they had spoken to her in such a manner. She was at a loss as to what to do, but she did know she and Mike were going to discuss his language and attitude toward the Sabbath, particularly her observance of it. *This is a conversation we'll have face-to-face.*

She knew she could write a brilliant article, and eventually Mike would forgive her and his outburst would be forgotten, but it would mean putting aside all her beliefs that Sunday was a holy day reserved for worship, service, and family. She might gain Mike's forgiveness, but could she forgive herself, and more to the point, would God forgive her if she broke the commandment to keep the Sabbath Day holy?

Carrie had thought Mike understood her commitment and her reasons, but his parting shot had proven that he really didn't. He was just humoring her and playing along. If he could ask her, no demand of her, that she break a commandment that easily once, then he could do it again. In fact, he might take it to mean that she had agreed to drop their arrangement permanently. No, she had to stand firm and stick to her beliefs; there wasn't a choice at all.

Sitting at the table, Carrie considered the consequences of her refusal. It would probably mean losing her job. If that was the case, then so be it. She would either get another job in the city or return to Utah, back to her family home. Another path would present itself to her, and she would follow it, always remembering her time in the city and the lessons she had learned there and relationships she had developed.

As she warmed some milk to make some hot chocolate, her favorite comfort food, Carrie had an idea. She wondered if it was pushing the boundaries too far and decided to pray for guidance. After rising from her knees and finishing making her soothing drink, she sat back down at the kitchen table, giving her one and only option more thought. A sense of peace washed over her, and she took it to mean her idea was acceptable.

Technically, Sunday ran from midnight to midnight. She always ensured she was at home by midnight, no matter what she was doing on Saturday night. This night was no exception; therefore, technically speaking, after midnight she could actually get to work and maybe make her deadline at 4 a.m. Problem solved. She decided to lie down for a while to rest and clear her head until it was time to begin writing at one minute after midnight. *Possibly not the spirit of the law, but definitely the letter of it.*

Carrie's alarm woke her at 12:01 a.m. She got out of bed, wrote the article, and breathed a sigh of relief as she hit the 'send' button. *Now Mike has his article. I'm going back to sleep.* She climbed back under the covers, turned off the lamp, and was off to sleep.

Walking into the office later that day, Carrie was confused to see Mike grinning at her as usual. She had expected him to still be mad at her, or at the very least give her the silent treatment.

"Great article, Carrie, perfect balance as always. I might just have to send you to the UK if they don't get the situation under control soon."

Carrie stared at him, bemused by the praise and his light tone. Seeing her face, Mike guffawed.

"Oh, you expected me to still be sore. That's not the New York way. I said what I had to say; you did what I needed you to do, and so we put it behind us and move on. You agree?"

"I guess so," Carrie replied, a little unsure that everything had been resolved that easily. "I did give you advance warning that I was turning my phone off though."

"Well, whatever, we'll let it go. Next time, make sure I'm actually listening to you and that you back it up in writing. At least I've cured you of your aversion to working on a Sunday."

Carrie shook her head. "No, you didn't, and it isn't an aversion; it's a tenet of my beliefs. There is no curing it and no getting around it. I stayed up until after midnight so I could begin work on the article in the early hours of Monday. If you can't accept that I need Sundays off to keep a commandment of God, I guess we need to address that right here, right now."

"You're feisty for such a cute little thing," Mike grinned. "Look, I'm sorry if I made you stay up all night and if I came on a bit strong, but you need to be tough to make it in this industry. You stood up to me, but you showed your dedication to the job by finding a way to complete the piece. Let's just go back to business as usual and call it a learning curve for the both of us."

Carrie knew that their unwritten agreement was now back in place and that Mike had said as much as he was going to about the matter of her beliefs. She'd gotten as much of an apology as she could expect from her gruff, hard-nosed editor, and it was good enough for her. She didn't like him calling her a 'cute little thing,' but she had learned to accept that it was just his manner and he spoke to all the women in the same way. It washed over her now that she knew him well, so she went back to work as normal, holding no grudges.

That afternoon Carrie found time to catch up with her correspondence, dismayed to find that Antonio had been concerned for her. Rather than taking the time to write, she picked up the phone and called him right away on his cell phone. If he was in a position to answer, he would; if not, she would leave a voice message to put his mind at rest.

"Antonio Dominguez," the strained voice at the other end answered.

"Hi, Antonio, it's Carrie."

Her stomach had filled with butterflies at the sound of his voice, and a huge grin had spread itself involuntarily over her face. She had no doubt he would hear it in her voice, and she hoped he would return it in his warm, dulcet tones.

"Carrie, thank the Lord above that you are safe and well. I half expected this to be the police or a member of your family informing all your contacts that something had happened to you."

He sounded distressed and relieved at the same time, and Carrie hurried to soothe him, explaining all that had happened over the weekend. She heard Antonio hiss with anger as she spoke of her telephone conversation with Mike, and she had to calm him down, assuring him that she loved her job and her boss wasn't normally so rude to her. The conversation drifted into easier areas and they chatted for an hour before Antonio had to hang up. He promised to call her back later.

Carrie passed the evening with dinner and followed up on other emails, replying to her family and Edith. She hesitated when she saw another email from Pete, but she clicked it open, not surprised to find he was following up on his request to meet up. He hoped she could meet him for an extended lunch on Wednesday. Like many tourists, he wanted to see the city from the observation deck of the Empire State Building and have a takeout lunch on a bench in Central Park. The outing sounded all too romantic for her liking, but she couldn't think of a way to word a refusal or suggest an alternative.

Before she could reply, she got lost in a daydream of doing the same things but with Antonio by her side, proudly showing him what was now her city, walking hand-in-hand around the well-known tourist spots and taking him to the hidden gems, arms wrapped around one another to hold off the biting New York wind, kissing on the bandstand in the park....

Whoa, just pull yourself up right there, girl, she told herself firmly. Those kinds of fantasies only lead to trouble, and in her case, would only lead to being more heartbroken when this came to an end. She wondered if she was wasting her life, spending all her time either working or keeping up with this completely impossible long-distance romance. Sure, some of her friends had been successful at distance relationships, even coast-to-coast relationships, but, really, an international relationship spanning an ocean?

Time and time again she had told herself she should break contact with Antonio, stop this madness, and give someone else a chance to enter her heart … and his. As much as she tried to apply logic to the situation, it was insurmountable. There was no room in her heart for another male suitor—it had been firmly chained and padlocked, the key handed to Antonio, and only he had the power to free it. When this ended, he would have to be the one to do it, and at that point, he may as well leave her heart chained up, because it would shrivel and die; God's love and her family's love would be her only comfort when it did.

Pulling herself together, Carrie wrote a quick message back to Pete, telling him she would check with her editor first thing in the morning and let him know if she could do lunch that day, but she would have to keep her phone on in case she was called back to work. She received an almost instant enthusiastic agreement, a bit too enthusiastic for her liking. She sighed as she turned off her laptop and relaxed while she waited for Antonio's name to pop up on her caller ID.

CHAPTER NINE

"Wow, what a view! Carrie, come and see this."

Pete held out a hand, hoping Carrie would take it so he could draw her closer.

"I've already seen it, and it is something, but I'm not that keen on heights. I'll just stay over here, thanks."

Carrie had no problem with heights at all. Her problem was Pete. He had spent the whole time in the line downstairs finding excuses to touch her. The crowds that always seemed to be waiting at the attraction didn't help, as they were sandwiched together in the long line. As much as she could enjoy his company, he was spoiling the day by trying to make this something more than it was. Carrie decided she needed to set him straight as soon as they were back down on ground level. He had ignored all her hints and subtle rebuffs and had backed her into a corner. Since she never liked confrontation, she didn't relish the thought, but this man needed to know that her heart was locked tight as a drum and belonged lock, stock, and barrel to another man.

Having seen enough of the city view, they left the building and headed to a street vendor to pick up food to take to the park. After finding an empty bench, they began their lunch as Carrie tried to turn the conversation to work.

"I'm so glad the Greenpeace issue has been resolved. It's one thing for individuals to have their beliefs and boycott the merchandise if they choose. It's quite another for the produce to spoil in trucks before they even reach the outlet that purchased them."

Pete nodded his agreement. "I know, it was ridiculous. They couldn't see that they were hurting the British retailers, not the Spanish producers. The goods had already been paid for, and the losses by the larger supermarkets that bought in bulk were devastating."

"You wrote some good articles on that, Pete. I was impressed. I'm sure that they helped the people see the financial aspect of it more clearly and helped end the situation. My editor was threatening to send me over to Britain if it didn't resolve itself soon. As much as I would love to do more international trips, Britain at this time of year might not be one of them. It's just too cold, especially hanging around highways."

Pete laughed along with her. "Yep, we want more trips like the Spanish one, much more romantic, eh? It's a shame you were kept back by the prince that night; it was still early, and I'm sure we could have found something exciting to do in Madrid together."

"I was actually thrilled that I was kept back. Nothing could have been more exciting than that."

"Well, you did get some great articles out of it, and it was a major coup for your paper, but spending all that time with that stuffy, pompous, stuck-up politician couldn't have been much fun."

"Antonio is not stuffy, and he's certainly not pompous or stuck up!" Carrie declared hotly, her cheeks flaming. "He's absolutely charming, fun to be with, and the most caring, down-to-earth person I have ever met, despite his upcoming titles and roles."

"Come on, Carrie, you're not writing one of your articles now. You don't have to keep up the fake admiration for that family."

"It's not fake, Pete. I got to know Antonio really well, and I admire him very much. He is truly a good man, and he's going to be a great leader."

Pete looked at her intently, seeing how her face brightened and her eyes sparkled as she spoke of the king-to-be. "Carrie, you don't want some patsy who can repeat the company line verbatim. You need someone who can think for himself, where the relationship can be a real meeting of minds. You need someone who truly understands what being a journalist means, someone who can travel the world with you on assignments."

"Someone like you, you mean?"

"I had hoped for that, yes. We got on so well the night we met, we just clicked, even in the most formal of situations. I thought you felt the same."

"Pete, I'm sorry, but I don't feel that way. You were good company that night, and if I gave off signals to say otherwise, I apologize, but I don't see us in a romantic relationship at all ... not ever."

"It's him, isn't it? Tell me it isn't. Surely you of all people weren't taken in by that oily, sleazy charm! I had you pegged as being a lot smarter than that."

Pete was getting angry, his face twisted into a sneer as he spoke.

"I don't need to listen to this," Carrie said. She stood and dumped her practically untouched lunch in the trashcan, gathering her things to leave.

"Oh my, you did, didn't you? The oh-so-innocent, prim little Carrie fell for the handsome prince. What else did he give you other than the stories? What did you trade for them?"

"How dare you!" Carrie exploded. "Pete, when I met you, I thought you were a nice guy, clever and interesting. You were very courteous and gentlemanly that night, and I thought we could be friends. I see I was very wrong, on all counts."

Carrie marched away only for an angry Pete to whirl her around, grabbing her arm so hard she was sure it would be bruised. "Don't think for a minute that you mean a thing to him. He'll drop you just as quickly as he dropped the other hundreds he's bedded. A commoner like you will never be anything other than an easy distraction for him before he's forced to marry some other blue-blooded snob and pop out suitable heirs by the dozen."

Carrie pulled her arm away and hurried from the park, heading back to her office. She could feel the bitter sting of angry tears in her eyes but refused to let them fall. *Why do people have to be so horrible to each other?* That was twice now in as many days that someone had used cruel words to cut her to the quick, and Carrie didn't understand why. The people she had grown up around and mixed with back home didn't play games, and they didn't set out deliberately to hurt other people. She was used to a much more gentle approach, with honesty and openness.

She had to admit to herself that the words hurt so much because of the truth within them. She didn't need anybody to tell her she had been a fool to fall for Antonio, or that it couldn't go anywhere.

Carrie had no idea about the allegations Pete had made twice now that the prince was a womanizer. She found it hard to believe of the upstanding man she knew, but it was a possibility, she had to admit. If so, Carrie wouldn't be the one to judge him; that right was reserved for a much higher power. *Judge not that yet be not judged.*

Pete also hadn't gotten to know her enough to realize she wasn't sleeping with Antonio. Surely if he only wanted a distraction, he would choose someone a lot closer, someone who would be willing to provide that kind of entertainment. She decided there was no point in torturing herself further with these thoughts, and she didn't want to empower his weaknesses by giving Pete— that nasty piece of work—the satisfaction of dwelling on his words. She put it out of her mind for the rest of the afternoon.

That night, Carrie called her mother, hoping to talk everything through with her for the first time since she'd called her from Madrid to share the news about her fairy tale night in the beautiful blue gown in the palace. Her mother listened patiently through the whole story, letting her daughter get it all off her chest, cry where she needed to, and laugh when she wanted to.

"You should have come to me sooner, Carrie. It sounds like this is more of a pickle than your usual dating disasters."

Carrie rolled her eyes. Her failed love life wasn't just known to her friends; she was close to her family and her mother was well in on the joke. She hoped that referring to it would lighten the mood and cheer her daughter up a little. Carrie chuckled a little through her sniffles. "I'm in deep this time, Mom, and I know this fairy tale will never end up happily ever after."

"So I see. Well, there really isn't much that you can do about it. You can't walk away, so the situation will just have to play out. The only comfort is that this is part of the path you need to walk; there is something here for you to learn, although it is never obvious when dealing with heartache. One day you will understand, and until then, trust Him to lead you and know that all things work together for our good. I promise you will see His tender mercies at play here."

"I know, and I am trusting that He will see me through."

Carrie knew that her mother had found the unexpected death of her husband very hard to deal with, being left with four daughters and a son, all teens and younger, to raise on her own as well as the massive empire that was Carpenter Global Press to run by herself.

She had never once drifted from her faith, even during that horrible time, and Carrie felt it was a true testament of how much her faith meant to her. She hoped she could always have that same strength and courage in her convictions. Her mother was talking again, and Carried pulled herself back to the conversation before she missed anything with her musings.

"As for the womanizing bit, if you care, I'm sure it can be easily checked out. Listen, I'm not entirely certain, but I think your sister mentioned some unofficial biography she was considering publishing that could help. I remember because we argued about it. I didn't think it was suitable, too much of an exposé rather than a serious work, but she told me, as usual, that I was being a prude and that for the business to thrive, I needed to lighten up and broaden my horizons."

Carrie laughed—that was so typical of Courtney. She wasn't really a blood sister, she was actually her cousin, but when her mother's sister Lucy had succumbed to a long illness, Courtney had only been seven and needed a family. Courtney's father, David, had gone to pieces when his wife got sick and died. He turned to alcohol to get through the pain. He had been in no fit state to care for a seven-year-old, so Carrie's parents had taken her in and loved her as much as their own. The entire family loved Courtney. Carrie always thought of her as a sister rather than a cousin, and that became official when David had shown no signs of pulling himself together and made no attempt to contact his daughter, quickly agreeing to the Carpenters' petition for adoption.

When Lucy and David married, David would have no part of attending the Mormon church, so Lucy stopped going as well. This meant Courtney was raised differently from the other Carpenter children and didn't have the same religious training. Once her mother died, her father left her, and the Carpenters adopted her, Courtney had been angry and rebellious. The last thing she was going to accept was religion being thrust on her when she was bearing the pain of losing her mother and, for all intents and purposes, her father as well. She blamed God for taking her mother away from her.

The Carpenters had tried to let her ease into the family activities, loving her regardless of her choices. "Why don't you give her a call? I'm sure she said it was the Spanish royal family. She'll have read it in detail if she was thinking of offering the author a publication deal."

"That's a great idea; it might be interesting to learn more about the family if I can stand to read it! And it's been too long since I've gossiped with my little sister."

"Might as well know one way or the other. What you find might give you the courage to walk away from your fairy tale prince."

As usual, Carrie felt much better when the call with her mom ended. She decided to give Courtney a call at the CGP office, but she was disappointed to learn the book was about the previous royal family, in particular King Juan Carlos. They hadn't been royal by bloodline and so were no relation to Antonio, who was of the family the Spanish considered the real royals—the ones that would have always held the throne if it hadn't been for civil war.

"I'll tell you what, though; I'm an absolute demon when it comes to sniffing out scandal online. Leave it with me for a day or two, Carrie, and I'll come back to you. If there is anything to find out about this guy, I'll have it by then."

The two girls chatted for a while longer, catching up on each other's news and promising to get together soon. *Hmmm...still no love interest in Courtney's life worth talking about.*

When Carrie hung up, she decided there was one more call she had to make; she dialed Susan's number. At first her friend had been outraged at the way Pete had spoken to Carrie, but she soon began to make light of it, cheering her friend and blaming it on Carrie's renowned lack of luck with men.

"Wow, even for you this is a first. A date reduced to a street brawl and a food fight—you outdid yourself with this one."

"I refute that! No food was thrown, except into the trash, and we weren't on the street, we were in the park."

The girls giggled over the ridiculous scenario and the incident was reduced from mountain to molehill, chalked up to yet another of Carrie's disastrous dates for the girls to tease her about whenever they got together.

She wasn't altogether surprised when two days later she received an email from Pete, pouring out his heart in a sincere apology. He told her that before he had worked for the financial paper he had been a freelance war journalist, seeing a lot of frontline action, death, and pain. He explained that he had fallen in love during one trip and married a local girl, but visa problems had meant he'd traveled back and forth several times before finally having the papers to enable him to bring his wife home.

When he arrived to tell her the good news, he found she had been killed in the crossfire from rebel soldiers two days before. He added that he'd never really gotten over it but was aware it had left him with some issues. Carrie wrote back straight away, saying how sorry she was, and that while it was great that he opened up to her and it was a major step, he needed to seek some spiritual or professional help. She finished up by saying that he would be in her prayers and that she hoped he could find a way to move forward.

Over the next few weeks, Carrie managed to get her life back on an even keel. Courtney had called her back and told her there was nothing to indicate that the allegations of womanizing were true where Antonio was concerned. She could find nothing except one long-term romance that had begun in his teens but didn't work out. His frequent appearances at functions with Princess Nadine of Switzerland seemed nothing more than political expediency.

Things continued as before with Antonio—phone calls till the wee hours of the morning, gifts arriving almost weekly that were often fun and funny rather than expensive gifts, and emails that could have filled volumes. Between her work and Antonio, she barely had time for little else. Carrie was back to her normal, cheerful self.

That was until the day that a news ticker announcement flashed across her screen while she was hard at work, and the bottom fell out of her world.

"...Dominguez family to announce royal engagement..." the rapidly scrolling banner declared. *Did I read that right? No, that couldn't have been right.*

Suddenly she sensed Mike marching out of his office toward her. He walked straight up to her desk with a huge grin on his face. Now she could have no doubt she had read the ticker correctly.

"Go home and pack, Carrie. Marcia's booking you on the next available flight to Madrid as we speak."

"Mike, I can't go. You don't understand and there's no time to help you understand my personal reasons. Please just assign one of the others. There are several who would give their right leg—or more—to be on a plane to Madrid. I'm just not one of them!" She was so upset her voice was leaning toward the 'too loud' marker on the Carpenter family scale of loss of control; Mike's voice was already off the scale.

"It has to be you, Carrie," he yelled, "and I'll be darned after all the time you've spent at the palace and the coverage you've given them that I'll allow you to tell me no. Now pack your things, and I mean it. This is not a democracy we're running here. I'm your boss!"

Carrie noted the other journalists in the bullpen around her desk had stood to see what Mike was yelling about now. She felt physically sick and very near tears. She had worked so hard to steel her heart and avoid Antonio, the palace, and the royal family. "Does it really have to be me?" she asked rather meekly, trying once more to forge a crack in Mike's determination.

"Of course it does, I've told you that. Nobody else will get on so well with them. You're our inside man at the palace! You may just get another chance at a scoop. Now, for the *very* last time, move it if you want to keep your job! You've got two hours to get home, pack a case, and get to the airport for check in. We'll send you updates as they break so you know what's going on when you get there." *Inside scoop? I've had the inside scoop and what has it gotten me? An impossible relationship with enough heartache to last a lifetime, that's what!*

Carrie stood on trembling legs, threw some materials in her briefcase, and made her way to the taxi already waiting outside the building for her. It was times like this when she always turned to God for strength and peace. She prayed all the way home.

Carrie sat on the bed in her hotel room in Madrid with her laptop, checking to see what updates the office had sent. This time she dreaded the trip; however, she had felt peace as she prayed in the taxi on her way home to pack for the quick trip. She barely remembered the flight at all; it passed in a blur of frantic thoughts. Her Spanish was better now, and she had gone through the motions of check-in with no problem. At least she was familiar with the hotel.

She had insisted to Mike and Marcia that she would make her own way around this time, since she knew the city a little. She had no desire to have to make small talk with anyone, especially not the friendly Miguel who had chauffeured her around on her first trip. She had run the gauntlet of emotions since hearing the news, and now she felt empty, numb. She would do her job, report the news announcement, and get home as quickly as she could.

She couldn't believe there was no warning from Antonio about this, or at least an opportunity to refuse the invitation. But there wasn't, and she had already made up her mind she would attend the announcement, make her report, and immediately fly home.

A simple text message had reached her when she deplaned at the Madrid airport: 'Hope you are coming to Madrid so I can explain all the news.'

The news! Of course she had known all along that the future king would be required to choose a bride from a royal family whose connections would benefit his own. Love wasn't necessarily a prerequisite for such a match, merely good political connections. What a fool she'd been!

She would have to stand among hundreds of people and pretend to be delighted at his engagement, concentrating on doing a good job of recording the information to pass along to her readers, who would expect all the details artfully described as though they were present for the announcement themselves.

She wasn't sure how she was going to do it, but she had no choice. Carrie had known this day was coming; she should have prepared herself for it a little more. They had never made any promises to each other. She had no one to blame but herself. Reading that the announcement was to be made the next day at the royal palace, Carrie shut down her laptop, said her prayers, and went straight to bed.

She didn't want to think or feel anymore tonight, but it didn't seem to matter what she wanted. The thought crossed her mind and kept her awake. Both her mother and God had told her she would learn something from this experience. Just what was it that she was supposed to learn as she suffered a terribly broken heart as Antonio got engaged? Whatever it was she was supposed to learn, she would pay attention later. For now, she was just too numb to think or feel.

CHAPTER TEN

This time there was no way the announcement could be made inside the palace. Even its majestic halls and rooms wouldn't have accommodated the turnout. The official announcement was to be made from the balcony overlooking the courtyard, where large numbers of attendees would await the news.

There was an area cordoned off for press, and Carrie stood there now, feeling panicky and completely trapped, both by her emotions and by her sense of obligation to her employer. She was determined to choose 'fight' rather than 'flight,' but it would take every ounce of strength and courage to keep from breaking free and running back to the hotel.

Carrie was surrounded by people, the rest of the square seemingly occupied by every single person who lived in Madrid and the surrounding areas. It reminded her of the Vatican and papal announcements she had watched on television. The people had turned out *en masse* to hear the joyful news of their beloved royal family. Flags and banners were waving; everyone was in a fiesta spirit as they waited for the family to appear.

When the family came out in procession, Carrie wished she didn't have such a great view. First came King Benito and Queen Isabella, walking regally arm in arm, dressed to perfection, their faces beaming with delight. Carrie's heart jolted and her eyes pricked with tears as she saw Antonio following behind them. She angrily wiped the tears away, furious with herself for allowing this situation to develop. Princess Catalina and Princess Adelina followed Antonio with two guardsmen bringing up the rear. She forced herself to ignore how handsome and dashing Antonio looked in his formal dress, or how comfortable and relaxed he looked standing in front of such a large representation of his people, his family by his side.

The cheers of the crowd were deafening as the five stepped forward to the edge of the balcony, waving and smiling to their loyal subjects. As the king held up his hand, the cheering came to a halt, a hushed silence falling over the crowd as they looked up adoringly at their leader, waiting for him to speak.

"Thank you all for coming here today to share our delightful news, especially since you have to brave the November weather to do so."

The crowd went wild again, and the king needed to wave both hands up and down to silence them so he could continue.

"It gives me great pleasure to announce…" King Benito paused for effect, enjoying the moment of looking over the crowd hanging on his every word. "That the Crown Prince, the heir to the throne…."

Carrie truly thought she was going to be sick. *Why did he have to drag it out? Just get it over with already so I can get out of here and nurse my wounds in private like an injured animal.*

"…Prince Alberto of Monaco has asked for the hand of our eldest daughter Princess Catalina in marriage, and we are delighted to say she has accepted."

Wait, what? Carrie's face filled with confusion. *Did he just announce Catalina's engagement?*

The king was talking again, but Carrie didn't hear a thing he said. She stared at the balcony, her mind a whirlwind of thoughts. When she saw Princess Catalina step forward to address the crowd, she could be in no doubt. Once again Carrie didn't listen; she was watching Antonio. When she saw his eyes hunting frantically through the sea of faces in the press area as his sister delivered her official speech, she felt her heart lift from her shoes back into her chest. When he finally found her and their eyes met, his face broke out into a wide smile, and Carrie couldn't help herself. She burst into tears—a flood of them.

"Wow, you really are excited with the news, aren't you?" a journalist standing next to her teased, giving her a playful nudge. She was too busy laughing and crying at the same time to be able to respond. She completely missed the sharp look that Queen Isabella gave Antonio, and the look that passed between her and the king before he stepped forward to declare the rest of the day a holiday, and that paella fiestas were to happen all over town. He demanded everyone eat, drink, and dance in celebration.

With that the family retreated, Antonio giving her a discreet wave and a very private look before he disappeared inside. A few of the reporters standing close to her gave her very curious looks, but she was too happy to pay much attention to them. She didn't even notice when a few of them discretely snapped her picture with their smart phones.

The crowds began to disperse, although the members of the press corps were still stuck in their designated area until there was more room to move. A guard shouldered his way through them, heading for Carrie.

"If you would please, Miss Carpenter, follow me. I have orders to escort you inside the palace."

Carrie happily agreed, excited that Antonio had sent for her. This time, a flurry of photographs were taken as

Carrie moved through the parting crowd with the guard, heading for the palace entrance.

She followed the guard into the drawing room, then immediately spotted the chaise lounge that she considered her and Antonio's love seat. She turned quickly when she heard someone enter the room. It wasn't Antonio, it was Queen Isabella.

"Sit," the queen demanded as she seated herself across from Carrie. The queen wasted no time getting straight to the point as Carrie was filled with trepidation.

"I wanted to speak to you regarding this ongoing relationship you have with my son. I have nothing against you personally, at least not yet, because I don't know you. Still, I feel I must explain some things to you. While arranged marriages are not law here, it is different for royalty. We are expected to marry within our status, making matches for the good of the country or to produce heirs with the correct bloodline. I am sure you can understand this. Love, or whatever else my son thinks he might feel for you, doesn't factor into it at all."

Carrie opened her mouth to speak, to explain that she did understand, but the queen silenced her with a raised hand as she continued.

"This dalliance can go no further. The only thing it can hope to achieve is to ruin my son's reputation. I didn't miss the glances that passed between the two of you today, and I'm certain that since there were hundreds of members of the press in attendance, at least a few of them didn't miss it either.

No doubt they will report on this tomorrow, dragging my son into a scandal, which he has so far avoided all his life. You know the industry, and I'm sure you can imagine how your colleagues will handle this. Spain is still in a delicate position right now; we had hoped that the engagement would overshadow the memory of the recent disaster and allow everyone to move on. It appears they will be moving on to a new story after all, just not the one we had hoped.

Please, I am appealing to you as both a queen and a mother who loves her son. Deny the allegations that will be put to you, say you became good friends during your coverage of the oil spill and nothing more, and walk away. Go home to America, and forget about Antonio, for his sake and for the sake of Spain."

With that, the queen rose and swept out of the room, leaving Carrie feeling very small. As soon as she composed herself, she rushed from the palace and walked the short distance back to her hotel. With every street she walked down, parties were in full swing; on several occasions, people with laughing eyes and happy smiles tried to coax her to join in, dancing in front of her, grabbing her and swinging her around exuberantly. She managed to raise a small smile and an apology to each person as she hurried away, desperate to get back to the sanctuary of her hotel room.

Arriving there, she flung herself onto the bed to cry. Finally she was able to compose herself and moved to the desk to write the article she was obliged to submit, relieved that she'd had her recorder running the whole time since she had missed so much of the announcement. The words had been hard to make out over the rowdy crowd and her emotions.

Now she needed both her ear buds and a lot of concentration to hear the recording. This was a good thing, because it kept her mind off the whole situation and the terrible meeting with the queen. Finally hitting 'send' to get her story on its way and removing her ear buds, she heard her phone beeping to indicate she had a text message. Opening it to read, she saw it was from Mike.

"Office inundated with calls and questions about affair with prince. Can't get you on phone, no reply to email. What's going on?"

Carrie fingered a short reply and hit send. "Coming home, see you soon."

She had packed and left the hotel within the hour, reaching the airport by the skin of her teeth to catch a departing flight with her open ticket. During the flight, she'd had no choice but to confront Queen Isabella's words in her mind. If she had the room, she would kick herself. She had been so busy enjoying the relationship with Antonio, coming to terms with how impossible it was, and how much it would hurt her when it ended, she hadn't even considered that it might have consequences for him, too—ones that affected his entire family ... his entire country.

The woman had been right—she was being selfish and she was hurting Antonio. It would break her heart to walk away, to shun him and push him out of her life, but it was what she needed to do. She had hoped that when it came down to this, it would be Antonio who would be the strong one, but it was obvious now that it needed to be her, and sooner rather than later.

Arriving back in New York, she headed straight to the office, suitcase in tow. Despite the ridiculously early hour, she found Mike in the office, exactly as she suspected. By the time she had finished telling him the whole story, the office was buzzing, the phones were ringing, and Mike's assistant had arrived with the morning's paper run. Carrie looked on, horrified at the headlines.

The Prince and the Pauper
Prince Shuns Sister's Speech for Mystery Blonde!
Ma, He's Making Eyes at Me!
Queen Looks on as Prince Flirts With Press!

Many of the articles were accompanied by pictures of Carrie's tear-stained face, or with Antonio's smoldering glance toward her before he left the balcony. She saw for the first time Queen Isabella's sharp features glaring at Antonio. Carrie put her head in her hands; it was worse than she thought. It was typical that the less scrupulous American press would be more interested in her involvement than the engagement of royals from other countries. This was terrible! She looked fearfully up at Mike through her lashes, afraid to raise her head.

"Right folks, damage control here! This could turn out to be good for the paper if we handle it the right way. Suggestions?"

Carrie sat in silence as everyone brainstormed over the best way to use this. And Mike; Mike was exploiting her broken heart into something that would be good for the paper regardless of her feelings.

All she wanted to do was crawl into her apartment and hide until it all went away. Her cheeks burned with shame as everyone discussed her personal life. She didn't even want to read the articles; she knew from the headlines how bad they would be. She had dragged both their family names through the mud, and she had no idea how to handle this.

Eventually, Mike came to his conclusion. "Carrie, you need to address this yourself. It will work far better than just ignoring it and letting it die down. Just think of the readership if we announce that you're going to respond personally! I suggest you do what the queen says, deny a romance, and say you are good friends. Hard to deny that look," Mike waved the picture of the prince in her face, "but if anyone can spin it, you can."

"I can't. I can't lie to my readers. I can't trivialize what I feel for him, and I can't spin this just so it gives us a great rating." She really resented that Mike was asking such a thing of her.

Mike nodded. "Well then, kiddo. I guess you're just going to have to tell the truth."

Carrie nodded and headed to her desk, opening a blank page on her laptop.

It took nearly six hours, but finally it was done. Carrie stared at the type on the screen, the letters blurring in front of her eyes. It told a deeply honest account of events, revealing far more of herself to complete strangers than she would ever want. It explained how she had met the prince during coverage of the environmental disaster, had been one of many invited to continue the conference at dinner, and explained the prince's reasons for asking her to stay behind that night and his subsequent offer to remain with him, exclusively covering the story.

She admitted how attractive she found him, and how she had fallen in love as they spent the time together. She informed the world that the relationship wasn't physical, due in part to her religious beliefs, and that the most the prince could be accused of was a friendship with an American.

She didn't mention the long hours they spent on the phone or the countless emails and small gifts they had exchanged through the months; merely that they had kept in touch after her return to the States. She didn't slur the family more by mentioning the meeting with the queen, only that she realized she could never be a part of Antonio's life and accepted that, but enjoyed his friendship while they had the opportunity.

It was an emotional piece, exposing herself and her feelings completely. She was reluctant to run it, but knew she had to clear the prince of the allegations lodged against him, ensuring it didn't jeopardize his position as the heir apparent or for a future marriage. Sighing deeply, she hit the keystrokes that would send it to Mike and went to the ladies' room to wipe her tears.

Ten minutes later, Mike dashed out of his office. "Carrie, this is fantastic. It's the best piece you've ever written. The readers are going to love it! Go home and get some sleep, take a couple of days off, and when you come back it'll all have blown over."

Carrie did as she was told. Feeling like a robot she left the office and headed straight home. She wanted to crawl into bed, but her answering machine was full of messages and was beeping incessantly. Pressing the button, she quickly hit delete on any that were from the press, TV stations, and Antonio. She didn't even want to hear his voice; she couldn't bear it. The only ones she listened to were from friends and family. She figured she owed her mom and Susan a call at least. They could get in touch with the rest, giving them a heads up about the upcoming article. They deserved to be forewarned.

Duty done, Carrie crawled into bed and let the jetlag carry her off into the comfort of a deep sleep. She knew it would take those two days off to get her emotions under control so she could once again step back into the world with her head held high.

CHAPTER ELEVEN

Come January, the world felt bleak and dreary as the city returned to normality after the jolly atmosphere, decorations, and joy of the holiday season. Just as Mike said, things had died down by the time Carrie had returned to work. Her article had left the gossips with nothing more to speculate over, putting a halt to the stories at this end and increasing her fan base even more.

After the fallout she had been nicknamed 'The People's Voice,' and she felt honored by the gesture of the readers and the other journalists who had picked up the term. She guessed that Antonio had been badgered at the other end, but she had seen nothing to indicate that the royal family had responded in any way. Like the articles, that chapter of her life was over.

Carrie had stuck to her word and had avoided all contact with Antonio for months, screening her calls, blocking his emails, deleting his texts and voice messages without opening them. It was for the best. She had managed to spend a few days at home over the holiday season, and back in the bosom of her family and her childhood church, she had come to terms with events. She knew that she would never love another as she had loved Antonio, that marriage and children weren't part of the plan for her. Surrounded by love, she could accept that and content herself with the amazing blessings she did have in life. There were many, and she felt lucky to have them. She would never be over Antonio—she would always love him, miss him, and long for him—but she could also carry on with life; it was the best she could hope for now.

She was mildly surprised when in February she was required to report on the engagement between Princess Nadine of Switzerland and Prince Lukas of Belgium, but she knew it made no difference to her situation. It didn't change any of the core issues. She treated it as any other news article, trying not to allow it to make her think of Antonio too much.

It was mid-May when Mike received the embossed letter addressed to him at the newspaper office. He immediately marched with it to Carrie, who barely glanced up from her screen.

"What's that?" she asked absently, as she continued to type.

"An invitation," Mike said proudly.

"That's nice; invitation to what?"

"Carrie, stop typing for a minute and pay attention to me."

Carrie stopped and turned her attention to Mike, noticing for the first time the thick, creamy quality of the paper and gold embossing of the letter he had been waving in front of her face.

"Very classy, must be something important."

"I don't know how important it is, but it's an invitation to a press conference." Mike paused and Carrie's eyes narrowed; he was acting cagey, and she didn't like it. *An invitation to a presser on embossed stationery? How weird is that?*

"Where?"

"The royal palace in Madrid."

"Don't. Even. Ask. I'm not going. Send someone else!" she said, returning to her document.

"I can't. It specifies you by name as the only individual invited."

"Tough."

"Oh, come on, you can't pass this up. They've sent out specific invitations. That means they've hand selected who they want to be there. That's a big deal, and we can't let ourselves not be represented."

Carrie rolled her eyes and rubbed her face with her hands. "So what's it about?"

"I don't know, it doesn't say, and there's been nothing on any news feed that I can find. Whatever it is, they're keeping it very hush-hush. My guess is that the king is announcing his retirement and handing over the crown. Come on, you have to be there. The readers will want your take on it. The People's Voice, remember?"

"I guess so," she muttered. "When is it?"

"In two days. My suggestion is you leave tomorrow and spend the rest of the day and night in the hotel so you're fresh for the morning conference. It's at 10 a.m. in front of the palace again."

"Must be big then, they're expecting a massive turnout. All right, I'll go. There doesn't seem to be much choice."

"Good girl," Mike said. "Leave any time to get organized; Marcia will get you on the earliest flight in the morning."

"Fine," Carrie said as she turned back to her computer.

As Carrie flung herself sulkily onto the giant bed in the hotel room, she told herself she was royally sick—no pun intended—of that journey across the ocean, and despite the elegance and beauty of the Westin Palace

Hotel and the royal palace, she never wanted to see either of them again in her life. She couldn't understand why this kept coming back to haunt her. The queen made it clear she was to stay away, so how could she receive an invitation to return?

She was using every ounce of her strength to ignore the continued communications she still received daily from Antonio, yet she kept being thrust into his world, his proximity threatening to break her resolve even months after her article putting it to rest. This had to be the last time, even if it meant giving up her career—or at least her job at *The Daily New Yorker*. She couldn't cope with it again. Every time she saw him, every time she went home, she left another piece of herself behind, another chunk of her heart ripped out and left bleeding on the runway as the plane lifted high into the air. Enough was enough!

She was cheered up to find an email waiting for her when she booted up. It was from Edith and she clicked to open it, hoping that the woman was coming for this announcement. She found the message said just that— that she would be arriving early afternoon that same day and hoped that Carrie would be there to get together for dinner. She wrote back to her quickly, telling her she was already there and to give her a call as soon as she was settled. Putting aside her laptop, feeling a sense of relief that she wouldn't have to face this alone, she lay down on the bed and took a nap; she still hadn't mastered the art of sleeping on a plane.

Her ringing phone woke her, and she squinted to see the time. It was four o'clock in the afternoon; she had slept much longer than she had expected. Picking up her phone, she checked the display before answering and was pleased to see it was Edith. She wasn't going to be hoodwinked into another meeting with the queen, that was for sure! She wouldn't be accepting any invitations into the palace on this trip.

She answered the call and greeted Edith warmly. In her no-nonsense way, her friend arranged to meet Carrie at 6 p.m. in the foyer so they could catch up. Hanging up, Carrie yawned, stretched, and headed for the shower.

"I must say, you had quite the time of it last year, didn't you?"

The women were sitting on a low, sleek cream sofa in the opulent foyer. Edith's coffee and Carrie's hot chocolate sat in front of them on a marble coffee table with gilt legs.

"It wasn't exactly the glittering highlight of my career."

"On the contrary, I would say it was," Edith protested. "You basically turned around, declared the truth, and shut the whole world up. It was really quite magnificent."

Carrie laughed. "It sure didn't feel magnificent! I was utterly mortified. My family is quite high profile back in my hometown. Obviously nothing to compare to the Dominguez family, but still, I felt I hurt them and was afraid the business would suffer too."

"What business are they in?" Edith asked, taking a sip of her coffee and wiping the froth moustache from her face.

"Publishing."

"Wait, hang on, Carpenter. Oh, not Carpenter Global Press?"

"That's the one," Carrie answered with pride.

"Gosh, Carrie, they're humungous! I had no idea. So how come you're slumming it as a journalist instead of running the family business?" She winked at Carrie, letting her know her words were in jest, but the question was a serious one.

"I don't know really, I was just drawn to journalism. I love to write, and although I knew I could get a publishing deal for novels easily enough, I just didn't feel

I would give enough doing that. It would come too easily, considering who the publisher would be. I felt I could do something as a journalist, help make the world a better place somehow. Silly, I guess."

"Nonsense! You can and you have. An admirable decision, especially with so many doors already open for you. It's a tough business, especially for a woman. Cry sexual equality and equal opportunities all you want, glass ceilings will always exist in many industries, and in the case of journalism, those ceilings are often about three feet high."

The women spent a very pleasant night together, and Carrie finally experienced the famous dining room for the first time. The food was excellent, the service impeccable, and the company great. Edith didn't revisit the subject of Carrie and the prince, allowing her to set the nature of the conversation. Neither could believe it when they noticed it was almost 11 p.m.

"Look at the time! I can't believe it's so late."

"Well, it's supposed to fly when you're having fun. I suppose we should call it a night, big day tomorrow. Are you going to be okay, Carrie?"

"I'll survive," she grinned at Edith. "Come out fighting at the other end as always."

"That's my girl!"

They hugged warmly and arranged to walk to the palace together in the morning. Saying goodnight, they headed for their rooms. After her long nap earlier and her body clock haywire with the time difference, Carrie didn't feel sleepy. She got ready for bed, then snuggled down to turn on the television. Flicking through the channels, she found she was definitely not in the mood for a tale of romance. This whole situation had certainly cured her of that addiction! *No more fairy tales and happily-ever-afters for this gal. Susan was right!*

Settling on a nature documentary, she blankly watched the screen flicker and the program change several times before she finally fell asleep.

The morning was bright and clear and the two journalists strolled to the palace. March was a pleasant time in Madrid. The sun was strong, creating a warm but pleasant day since it was still several weeks away from the sticky humidity of summer. It had been eight months since Carrie first came to Madrid.

Carrie in her black business suit and Edith in her tweed felt quite comfortable as they enjoyed the pleasant walk. Carrie was nervous, of course, wondering how she was going to react when she saw Antonio. *Maybe this was completely unrelated and he wouldn't even be there.* She knew it was a vain hope, but she was adamant she could steel her heart to handle it and hold her head high. Most of the speculation within the journalistic community had revolved around King Benito handing over the crown. Despite her fears, Carrie walked tall. She had two dear friends walking by her side today—God and Edith—and with their help, she would get through this.

Reaching the palace courtyard, they were once again escorted to an area front and center reserved for the press. This time, Carrie saw many more TV crews than newspaper reporters, including all the Spanish stations and many of the larger American news stations. She looked at Edith, who shrugged, as puzzled as Carrie by their presence; the Europeans they could understand, especially the British who had a real soft spot for royals, but Americans? The same as last time, outside the designated area, crowds of Spanish people had gathered. She thought there might actually be more than last time, but it was hard to tell since they were all crammed together like sardines in a tin.

Carrie tried to focus on her surroundings, feeling herself becoming light-headed. She took a few deep breaths, then surveyed it all—the microphones at the podium high on the balcony, the expectant, cheerful faces of the crowd, children sitting high on their father's shoulders, flags in hand ready to wave. She felt Edith's hand on her shoulder, giving it a firm squeeze, steadying her. She was almost afraid to look up as the crowd began to cheer and applaud. She heard directors' shouts of 'rolling' as anchors presented quick pieces to the cameras before the giant lenses swung round to focus on the balcony.

Carrie plucked up the courage to follow the cameras' one-eyed gaze, and her heart ached with longing as she saw Antonio, surrounded by his family, looking anxiously at the crowds. It was the first time she had seen him look uncomfortable in any situation, and the desire to run to him to reassure and comfort him was almost overwhelming. She had no time to wonder what was going on as the king stepped forward and silenced the people.

"My dear, loyal subjects of Spain," he began. "We have gathered here today united as a family because my son wishes to make a special announcement. May I present to you, Antonio Dominguez."

The crowd once again went wild for their favorite royal, welcoming him up to the podium with a response that lasted for minutes as Antonio raised first one arm and then both to ask for silence.

"I hope the words I am about to speak will receive the same reaction, for it is not an easy matter that I wish to discuss with you today. A few short months ago – eight to be exact - Spain had an international crisis, one for which we were criticized and even hated by some. Thanks be to God and those who offered their support and their aid! The crisis is over, and most of the world has forgiven us.

During that time, there was one woman in particular who turned her sympathy and understanding to our country, defending us against those who despised and blamed us, although it did not benefit her in any way to do so. This woman was a journalist from the United States called Carrie Carpenter, known in her country as The People's Voice."

Carrie stared up at the balcony in astonishment. *What's going on?* She looked frantically to Edith, who just chuckled and pointed back to the stage. Carrie turned to find Antonio's eyes boring into her, the intensity on his face unfathomable. A few of the Americans present had let out a small whoop as her name was mentioned, but the Spanish were silent, unsure of what was coming next.

"During the time that Carrie spent here reporting the crisis, she and I became very close, perhaps closer than we should have. I admit I admired her even before I met her because of her writing alone, and that admiration was intensified when I saw her beauty."

The crowd chuckled a little, men slapping each other on the back, proud of the fact that all hot-blooded

Spaniards had an eye for a pretty woman. Even Antonio couldn't prevent a barely-there smile from adorning his face when he saw their response.

"I have to confess, the more time I spent with her, the more I came to love her. At first, the situation seemed impossible. I had no doubt Queen Isabella would not accept an American journalist as the future ruler of Spain."

The crowd laughed aloud, delighted with the wry smile and the 'so-sue-me' shrug from their queen in response to the huge, cheeky grin Antonio turned sideways to give her.

"Of course, the papers got hold of the story and tried to start a scandal, as they have the tendency to do." Antonio took a moment to stare pointedly into the press enclosure, and Carrie could practically feel some of them shifting uncomfortably and trying to disappear from his scrutiny. "At this time, Carrie wrote her own story, a public declaration of her love for me, and put the idea of a scandal to bed before it had begun."

Carrie heard gasps from the crowd. She didn't care about the reaction of her fellow journalists; it was the reaction of the Spaniards that held her interest. She had no idea what Antonio was doing, but it was a relief to see many of the women clutch their hearts and mutter among themselves. It was all she had time to see before Antonio spoke again.

"My mother wasn't the only stumbling block in the relationship, of course." Antonio had to wait for the laughter and calls to die down before he could continue. "Although I know my family will come to love Carrie, and I think she would make a brilliant queen, I know this wonderful country and its people deserve to retain the traditions and history upon which it was built. It took so long for the royal bloodline to be restored to its true place, and it would not be fitting either for the country, for our people, or for us personally to stake a claim to that. Spain must remain true to its heritage."

The crowd went silent, the good humor fleeing and the party atmosphere becoming tense. Even the king and queen were beginning to look a little anxious. Antonio swallowed hard, and then continued.

"My question to you this day is this: Great people of Spain, will you forgive me if I step down from the position for which I was born? Will you understand if I renounce my claim to the throne, passing the responsibility to my dear sister, Adelina? Will you love and support her as you have done me, and my father before me?"

Antonio held out a hand behind him, the silence deafening as Adelina took his hand and stepped up to his side, looking every inch the royal princess fit to rule. She didn't flinch under the silence of the crowd; she stood strong and firm, awaiting their decision. Muttering began to spread through the crowd, the odd words reaching the journalists ears. Carrie understood only some of them, but she could clearly make out sacrificio por amor. *Sacrifice for love?*

It didn't take them long to make up their minds, although the wait felt like an eternity, both on the balcony and in the press enclosure. A smattering of applause broke out, which soon became a roar, and cheers and chants filled the square, Adelina's name being clear among them. The brother and sister on the stage began to smile, then grin, and Adelina waved to her people, thrilled to be accepted as the new heir apparent. She hugged Antonio, quietly thanking him for the opportunity and wishing him every happiness. As Antonio turned to the crowd again, they fell silent, but there was no menace in the atmosphere now.

"With the blessing of my family, and now the blessing of this representation of the people of Spain, I wish to return Carrie's amazing gesture and publically declare that I, Antonio Francisco Javier Carlos Dominguez, am madly, deeply, and passionately in love with Carrie Marie Carpenter."

Tears streamed down Carrie's cheeks as the crowd screamed their enchantment with the declaration. She barely noticed the cameras being turned on her, the flashing of photography from every direction. *He loves me! He loves me!* Although Carrie knew they still couldn't be together just yet, the very fact that he had publicly declared his love for her was enough. It soothed her soul and she knew this moment would live in her heart forever. She would forever draw strength from this amazing moment when Antonio declared his love for her with the approval of his countrymen.

Carrie followed along blindly as a guard lifted the cordon and indicated for her to duck underneath. She was hurried into the palace and up to the balcony before she knew what was happening.

As she saw Antonio front and center from the side of the makeshift stage, months of pent up emotions and carefully controlled feelings flooded out. No matter what the future held, this was their moment. She ran to him, and he caught her, swinging her high into the air and around and around, to the cheers of the exhilarated crowd. As he set her feet back down, he pulled her close, one strong, firm hand on her back, the other cradling the back of her head as he held it against his chest. He bent down, whispering softly in her ear, too low for the microphones to pick up.

"Carrie, in a few hours I am to be baptized. Will you join me in witnessing and celebrating my rebirth into your faith?"

Carrie pulled back, staring up into his face, dumbfounded.

"My faith?" she whispered, unable to believe all this was true. He nodded, his handsome face grinning at her.

"Now my faith, too."

Carrie felt like bursting into tears all over again, but she had been crying so long, no tears would come. Instead, she broke into a smile so wide she could barely form words around it. "Of course I will!" she managed to gasp out.

Antonio's face became serious again. He stepped back from her and the people hushed, aware that something more was about to happen. She could hear the whir of camera lenses refocusing over the stillness as Antonio went down on one knee before her. He pulled a small, velvet box from his pocket, opening it to reveal an exquisite ring with one large sapphire surrounded by what seemed like a million sparkling diamonds.

"Carrie Carpenter," he intoned gravely in his smooth, rich, baritone voice. "I can no longer offer you a kingdom or great riches. All I have to offer is my heart, and hope that it is enough. Will you do me the honor of becoming my wife?"

"Antonio Dominguez," Carrie replied, playing to the crowd and the watching world, following his lead. "Your heart is everything I have ever wanted. No matter your position in life, you will always be my king. Yes, I'll marry you."

Antonio slipped the ring on her finger and stood to hug her, while the people crowded into the square and the streets beyond cried, hugged, kissed, danced and sang. Adelina rushed in to hug them both before the king and queen stepped forward to welcome Carrie officially into the family.

"I hope you like the ring; I chose it because the sapphire is the exact shade of blue as your eyes," Antonio whispered to her among the commotion of celebration, as he stood with one arm around her shoulders, the other waving to the crowd.

"I love it, and I love you."

Antonio turned her from the crowd to face him, his head bending to kiss her, pausing before he did so. "Just don't break it. It's a precious family heirloom, a priceless antique."

He winked at her and postponed the kiss as Carrie burst into hysterical giggles. She just couldn't take this all in. *Things like this don't happen in real life, do they?* Especially not to ordinary people like her. She stared at him, taking his face in her delicate hands, making sure he was real, this handsome prince who had given her the fairy tale moment she had dreamed of all her life, her king who had sacrificed everything for love.

The singing and dancing crowd as well as the watching eyes of the world's press faded away for both of them as they sealed their lives together with a kiss so deep, it felt it would last a lifetime. When the kiss finally broke, they walked slowly from the balcony, entwined around each other, leaving behind the crowds, leaving behind Antonio's old life as they headed toward a new one. Together.

NOW AVAILABLE!

Sanctuary, Chelsea's Story
The Carpenter Chronicles, Book Two

In bookstores and on Amazon in
paperback and ebook.

**IT'S NOT LOVE THAT HURTS, BUT THE LOSS OF
LOVE.**

Chelsea Carpenter learns of her fiancé's death in Iraq
while choosing her wedding dress, just weeks before
Clark was due home. Her 'happily-ever-after' was not to
be. She could never love again.

Devastated and broken-hearted, Chelsea tries to escape by throwing herself into her work at the Carpenter family's publishing business, the only other love of her life aside from her family. Before and after work she hides herself away in a condo in the mountains above Sundance where no one stops by to interrupt her self-imposed exile from the world. She only ventures out to attend church, pick up groceries, and see her family. They worry that after two years she still cannot move on, but are helpless to find a way to bring her out of her shell. If anyone can do it, Carter, her twin brother can.

Just imagine that you are a 26-year-old, beautiful publishing executive who has absolutely no interest in any man because you firmly believe your fiancé was your one and only true love in this life.

What would you do when situations continue to arise that throw you directly into the path of a new gorgeously handsome employee, one that makes your heart flutter and your palms sweat each time you see him? To acknowledge an interest in another man would be to betray your dead fiancé, right?

Now Available!

Salvation, Courtney's Story
The Carpenter Chronicles, Book Three

In bookstores and on Amazon in
paperback and ebook.

Now Available!

Survival, Carter's Story
The Carpenter Chronicles, Book Four
In bookstores and on Amazon in
paperback and ebook.

If you've enjoyed reading this book, I really hope you'll do me the honor of leaving some positive feedback on the Amazon sales page for it so other readers will know you liked it

Janice

For updates on coming releases,
sales and events for books by
Janice Limb Myers,
please sign up here:
http://JaniceLimbMyers.com

Support Christian Authors and Read Great Books:

Christian Books in Multiple Genres, Join Christian Indie Author ~ Readers Group on Facebook for opportunities to learn about more great Christian authors.

https://www.facebook.com/groups/291215317668431/